Captured

By

Ronna M. Bacon

Psalm 138:7

Though I walk in the midst of trouble, You will
revive me;
You will stretch out Your hand
Against the wrath of my enemies,
And Your right hand will save me.

NKJV

Table of Contents

Chapter 1

Her hands clenching the rail on her back deck tightly, Suzanna Walters stared around, fear in her heart. She had been back at work as a detective with the Riverville Police Force for a few months now, after almost losing her life to a bullet. She and others had been ambushed trying to transport a prisoner into the courthouse. She still felt fear every time she headed there. She kept to the office as much as she could. Counselling had been offered and she had tried it, not finding it helpful.

She sighed to herself, pulling her honey-blond hair back into its usual ponytail, her soft brown eyes searching the area. For some reason she felt threatened and followed but could see no one. She wasn't ready yet to talk to Caleb Logan, the police chief, but if it continued, she knew she would have to.

Sue walked through the police department building, greeting her fellow officers, before she unlocked her door and then stared at the desk. No, she thought, the work has not done itself. I so hoped it would overnight. Already fatigued, she sank into her chair, her head bowing for a moment. God, they tell me You care. That You are everywhere. I've been searching, but I don't know if I have found You. I feel a peace at times that I know could only come from You. I know You love me. Please, Lord? Let me feel Your presence today. Thank you.

She looked up as she heard footsteps pause at her door. Frankie Brennan, a fellow detective, stood there, a thoughtful look on his face.

"Sue? What do you have on your desk right now?" He sat across from her.

"Too much." She shook her head as he grinned at her. "Why?"

"There's a course Caleb would like us to take. It's on family tree stuff. Micah's Kat is giving it."

"That sounds interesting. I've heard of it." She sat back, her eyes narrowed as the thought of getting away from her desk for a while went through her mind. "When is it?"

"Like, tomorrow?"

"Tomorrow?" She stared at Frankie as he grinned at her. "That's too much notice. We'll never be able to do it."

He laughed. "Apparently she has had a couple of cancellations and approached him."

Sue watched Frankie walk away before she sighed, her eyes on her paperwork. It was getting late, she knew, and finally just tidied her desk and locked her door, heading out for a walk. She needed that, she thought, not seeing Caleb watching her.

She paused by the gazebo in the park, not sure why, a frown on her face as she looked around. She could hear muttering but couldn't see anyone. A hand on her weapon, she walked rapidly towards the sound, eyes searching. A sudden yell from behind her had her spinning and then heading for the ground as a body

—

slammed into her. She landed heavily, the breath knocked from her body, before she was shoving at the male who had taken her down.

"Get off me." Her shoves had failed to dislodge the man. "Let me up."

"No. Stay down." She could feel his body moving as he looked around before he shifted away so that he could look down at her. "Did I hurt you?"

"No! Just move!" She scrambled back from him, eyes narrowing as she studied him. "What just happened?"

He shrugged. "I can't explain."

Sue's badge was out as she held it up. "Explain unless you want to be charged with assaulting an officer."

He paled as he stared at her before his mouth opened and closed and then he stuttered. "A police officer? Oh, man! Can my day get any worse?"

Sue stared at him for a moment. "Care to explain?"

His vision caught movement behind her and he reached to pull her to her feet. "Come on. We need to get out of here."

Sue pulled away from him, shaking her head. "Not until you tell me what is going on." She stopped short, feeling an arm come around her. "Back away."

The arm tightened around her and she felt her weapon pulled from her holster and then she was shoved forward, the man in front of her catching her before she went down. She spun, her eyes narrowing as she confronted the men in front of her.

"Let it go, lady. You're not the one we want. We want him." The shorter of the men had spoken.

"Not happening. Now, drop your weapons."

The men laughed, then moved towards them, causing them to step backwards.

"Turn around and walk towards the trees. Both of you."

Sue jumped at the harshness of the voice, a frown crossing her face. She knew that voice, didn't she? She just couldn't put a name to it. The man who had tackled her reached for her hand, his warm and strong on hers. He shook his head slightly as she glanced up at him, before they were forced to the side of the road and into a cube van, the door pulled down, shutting them into darkness.

Sue was on her feet, balancing herself as the van moved with the traffic, seeking an exit but finding none. She felt the man standing beside her.

"Okay, what is going on? And what is your name, anyway?" Her words were clipped, anger evident in them.

"I'm Graeme McDiarmid. New to Riverville. I paint and hang wallpaper. Nothing that would have anyone after me but they have been. Since I started this last project."

"And that would be? I'm Detective Sue Walters, by the way."

She heard him sigh before he spoke. "I was hired to do the painting in a heritage building on the outskirts of town. Those men have been around but today is the first they have approached me."

"Which building?"

"The MacKay homestead." He heard her indrawn breath. "Is that a problem?"

"It shouldn't be. There have been rumours circulating for years about it." Her hand came out to touch the van wall as she felt the vehicle stop. "Now, comes the fun. We need to get away."

"And I don't think we will." Graeme's dark blue eyes met Sue's brown ones as the light appeared from the opening door.

Graeme was pulled from the van, and as he struggled, a vicious blow from a bat took him down, the blood beginning to seep through his dark brown hair. Sue shoved at the man holding her.

"Let me go. I need to see to him." She felt her hands pulled behind her and bound, her badge and handcuffs removed.

"Not happening, lady. For now, you stay with us. You'll never be found."

She was shoved forward and down rough and broken steps, her shoes sliding at times. She felt herself shoved harder and into a damp, dark room, the only light from a small broken window. She heard rather than saw Graeme dumped beside her. She waited, feeling her bonds loosened and then a door slamming behind her. She waited, for what she wasn't sure, and then spun, running for the door and shaking it, finding she couldn't open it. Her hand rested on it, her eyes searching for anything, anything to use as a weapon, anything to use to get them out of there. She shot Graeme a look before she was back and on her knees beside him. He needs help, Lord, help I can't give him. Where are You? Sitting beside him, her hand rested on his chest, feeling the rise and fall of it as he breathed, not knowing how severely he was hurt. She sighed. Lord, You really didn't have to do this. Couldn't you have gotten my attention some other way?

Chapter 2

His hand on the door knob, Frankie twisted it, finding the door to Sue's office locked. That was strange, he thought. It was late afternoon of the next day. He had attended the seminar but Sue hadn't. He knew she had planned to be there. Kat, a good friend of hers, had asked where she was.

He turned, searching the building for her, before running for his car and heading for Sue's. He parked in her driveway, not seeing her car, which should have been there. He searched, not finding her, standing at the sliding doors to her kitchen, hands cupped around his face. She just wasn't there.

He spun, his phone out to call Sue. Having to leave a message for her just didn't work, Frankie thought. He headed back for the department. He needed to find Caleb.

"Caleb?"

Caleb turned at the sound of Frankie's voice, hearing his footsteps rapidly approaching him. He frowned.

"Frankie? What are you doing here? Is your seminar finished already?" He squinted at his watch. "How was it?"

"Interesting, to say the least." Frankie paused to catch his breath. "The thing of it is was that Sue never showed up. I didn't hear from her." He pointed over his shoulder. "Her door's still locked. Her home is locked up. Her car? It's still in the parking lot here."

Caleb stared at Frankie, a frown on his face. "The desk officer has a key to her office. Get it." His phone was out as he tried calling her, his call going to voice mail.

Frankie stood in Sue's office, a frown in place. She had tidied up and left for the day, he thought. He turned in a circle, not seeing anything.

"Did she have her purse, Frankie? Do you know?" Caleb stood beside him, doing his own assessment of the area.

"She never uses one for work. She told me that years ago. She keeps what she needs in a small wallet or folder and sticks that in a pocket." He rubbed his hand through his hair. "Now what, Caleb?"

"We look for her. Her phone is going straight to voice mail. It doesn't if she knows it's one of us. She's good that way." He turned, walking rapidly away, searching for officers he could free up to search.

The next morning, Caleb looked up from his desk, hope on his face as he saw Frankie in his doorway, his heart sinking as his friend shook his head.

"No sign of her, Caleb. She has disappeared into thin air. That's not her. Not anymore."

"No, I agree." Caleb's eyes dropped to the paperwork he had on his desk before he rose. "Where would she be?" He looked up as Eddie Brown, the most senior of the detectives, approached.

———

"Eddie? Somehow, I'm not liking the look on your face."

Eddie shook his head, a frown appearing. "We have someone else missing. A Graeme McDiarmid. He's a painter working out on the MacKay heritage home. The owner went looking for him this morning and couldn't find him. Graeme's truck is still there but there's no sign of him anywhere around."

"Another missing person?" Frankie stared at Eddie and then at Caleb. "Are they connected?"

Caleb shrugged. "Find out what you can about him, Eddie. Frankie, start searching around there. Take who you need with you." He looked around as his name was called.

"Caleb, this was just delivered." The desk officer handed him a plain brown envelope.

"Thanks, Joe. Who left it?"

Joe shook his head. "We didn't see. We're going back through the security footage, but it just appeared on the front desk."

"Let me know what you find." Caleb turned back to his office, studying the envelope before he was reaching for his letter opener. Dumping out the contents, he froze before his eyes raised to both Eddie and Frankie. Reaching for a pen, he opened the small black folder. "It's Sue's badge."

"Now, that's interesting. She wouldn't have done this. Someone has to have her, somewhere." Eddie frowned himself, and then walked away, deep in thought.

———

"Caleb?"

"I know, Frankie. I know. Where is she? Somehow, she's been taken captive. We need to start going through cases she's worked on." Caleb's eyes were on the wall opposite him for a moment. "Start your search on McDiarmid. It may be that this is related to that, but I don't see how at the moment."

Caleb looked up as Frankie and Eddie approached him in the break room the next day, their heads shaking at the question on his face.

"No sign of her, Caleb. No sign of McDiarmid, either."

Caleb was past them and at the front desk as he heard a commotion there. He stood, watching the young man who was there, agitation evident in his movement.

"Joe? What do we have?"

Joe turned. "He says he saw a man and woman being abducted the day Sue disappeared. He didn't think anything of it at the time but he's questioning if he really did see something now."

Caleb nodded. "Take him to one of the interrogation rooms. I'll send someone in to talk to him." He looked around, a finger pointing at Eddie. "Eddie, you talk to him. Frankie, you're with me."

"Where to, Caleb?"

"The gazebo. That's what I heard him say. Why would Sue be there of all places?"

Frankie's eyes slid closed as his steps slowed. "She likes to walk there. To think. Just to sit. How did I forget that?"

Caleb just shook his head as he walked rapidly that way. "We'll search, Frankie."

Thirty minutes later, Caleb bent to pull something from the shrubs. "Frankie? Handcuffs?"

"And I have a weapon. It's police issue, Caleb."

Caleb nodded. "Call for a team, Frankie. It looks as if Sue was here. And check the serial number of that with the list of our officers' weapons. We need to know if it is hers."

Chapter 3

A week later, Caleb walked once more through the park, his eyes searching, his heart raised in prayer for Sue. He knew she was just a young believer, not grounded like his friends had been who went through what they termed as their 'adventures'. He looked around as he heard a voice calling his name. Murphy O'Brien walked towards him. Murphy was one of the men who were on Rebel's Elite Security team, but more important, a good friend to himself and a friend of Sue's since college.

"Caleb? Any word?" Murphy jammed his hands into his jacket pockets. "Adriel's really worried. I was hoping we'd hear some good news."

"Nothing, Murphy. Not a sign of her. No ransom demand. This just doesn't make sense."

"Not, it doesn't. You said something about someone else missing?"

Caleb nodded. "There is. A Graeme McDiarmid. We're not sure how that connects with Sue."

"Graeme McDiarmid? I know him. Or at least I used to. I grew up with someone by that name." Murphy shook his head. "There's no way he'd be here in town."

"And why not?" Caleb searched Murphy's face. "Can you tell me why not?"

"He never wanted to leave his hometown. He loved it. He told me one time that was where he would die." Murphy groaned. "I didn't mean it that way."

"I know you didn't, Murphy. What did your friend do?"

"He was at college with me, earned his Bachelor of Arts. He was interested in painting and charcoal work." Murphy paused, a hand rubbing at his face. "I heard just after we graduated that his father took sick and he headed home to help." Murphy's voice died away as his thoughts drifted back in time.

"Murphy?" Caleb repeated his name, causing Murphy to shake his head and look at Caleb. "What did his father do?"

"He was a painter and wallpaper hanger. He specialized in heritage buildings. Why?"

Caleb's eyes slid shut as he groaned to himself. "The Graeme McDiarmid that's missing? That's what he does for a living."

Murphy stared at Caleb, finally remembering to snap his mouth closed. "So, it is Graeme. That's interesting. How does that connect with Sue?"

"That's what we're trying to determine." Caleb looked around, feeling himself watched. "Someone's out here, Murphy. I just wish we could find them. We don't even know if they're together or if their disappearances are separate and unrelated."

"Somehow, I think they're related. If I know Graeme as well as I used to, if he saw Sue in difficulty, he would step in."

"And Sue would step in as an officer if she had to." Caleb paused his steps, deep in thought. "Murphy, can Micah and Kat start a search on him? And talk to Emma. I know he's your friend, but we need to find out everything we can about him."

Murphy nodded. "I can do that. I know Emma started searching for anything on Sue, just as a matter of habit, I think." He turned to walk away. "Keep praying, Caleb. Sue's such a new believer."

"That she is." Caleb watched Murphy walk away and then turned, his steps halting as he saw the large brown envelope just in front of him. His eyes searched, not seeing anyone, before he pulled out a latex glove from his pocket and picked up the envelope, seeing his name printed in bold black ink. Who is doing this, Lord?

His steps stopping at his desk, he dropped the envelope, feeling like he was just repeating a day from his past. He slit the envelope open and dumped out the paperwork that was in it. A pen in hand, he sifted through it. Sighing, he reached for his phone, calling for a lab tech and then Frankie.

Frankie studied the paperwork. "What is this, Caleb?"

"I have no idea. I found the envelope in the park. Murphy and I had been talking. Neither one of us saw who left it. I checked with him. He's working on finding information on McDiarmid." He shook his head. "Apparently, he's a friend of Murphy's from his past."

"What? Did we know that?" Frankie rubbed at his neck. "I just wish we could find them."

Caleb watched as the tech sorted through the material and then stood back. "What did you find?"

"Nothing out of the ordinary, Caleb. Whoever sent this was very careful. Nothing I can find to track them or identity them. About what we figured."

"Thanks, Stu." Caleb reached for the paperwork, reading through it, staring at the photo he found. "Where is this, Frankie?"

"That's the old cement plant. The one that's abandoned on the edge of town." His voice died away. "You don't think?"

"Find Doug and his team. Send them out there, in civvies, I think. Go with them. It may be a wild goose chase but we have to follow it up."

Frankie was away, searching for Doug. Hurried conversation had Doug's ETF team scrambling for civilian clothing and then for vehicles.

Doug Foster studied the building. He knew it well. They did a lot of training here, he thought. Now, where would they put them?

"The basement, Doug." Tom Allison, second in command, stood beside him. "There are some rooms down there they could be locked in."

The men moved forward quietly, hand gestures in use when needed. Frankie followed Doug, his weapon in hand as they searched, moving through the building from top to bottom. They paused as they reached the basement, then crept forward on almost silent feet, stopping as they reached a door with a new lock on it. Glances were exchange before their feet hit the door, knocking it inward. They paused for a moment, their eyes searching before their gazes dropped to the floor.

"They were here, Doug. Where did they take them?" Frankie spoke for them all, seeing the disturbance on the floor. "We're too late."

Doug felt anger running through him. Sue was a good friend of theirs. Who had her, Lord? And just where is she now? Is she alive or dead?

Frankie turned, his phone out to call for the crime scene team, even as he reached for a metal object on the floor. An earring. Sue's, he thought. Yes, she was here, but where now?

Chapter 4

Sue had roused the day after they had been abducted, her eyes opening, and she sighed to herself. No, it's not a bad dream or a nightmare. I really am in this basement room, I'm cold, and tired and thirsty. What's the idea, Lord? Can't get my attention any other way?

She sat up, her eyes searching the room in the dim early morning light, her gaze landing on Graeme. She rose to walk across to him, dropping by his side, her hand on his face feeling for a fever. No fever, but he's still out. He needs to be in a hospital. But how do I get him there?

She rose once more, making a methodical search of the room, her eyes on the window before shaking her head. There is no way she'd get out there, let alone get Graeme on his feet and through it. It just wouldn't work. She paused at the door, her hand resting on it, before she twisted at the knob, feeling it turn under her hand but the door remained tight in its frame. She turned leaning against it before she once more searched the room, looking for anything that would help, and finding nothing. She knew the building, she thought. An abandoned one.

She slid to the floor, her back against the wall, muttering to herself, her eyes on Graeme. Just who is he, she thought? And why was he in trouble? Her

—

23

instincts kicked in and she rose, moving to search his pockets, finding nothing in them. But then hers were like that too, she had already checked. She frowned down at him. No, she thought, I don't know him, but I feel like I should. That I have seen him somewhere.

She didn't look up as the door opened and she heard movement coming towards her. She stared down at the bags that were dropped in front of her, refusing to look up. She felt herself shoved backwards, barely keeping her balance as the man stooped over Graeme, roughly rolling him to his back and assessing him. She watched closely, trying to remember his looks, as he shook his head and walked away, ignoring her comment that Graeme needed medical help.

She poked at the bags, not sure what was in them, or if she even wanted to open them. She finally undid them and peeked in. Water, she thought. Sandwiches, which I will never get down Graeme.

She reached for a water bottle, inspecting it and rubbing her thumb all over it. It didn't appear to be tampered with, she thought. She unscrewed the top and then reached to raise Graeme's head, forcing some water down him. Not enough, she thought. I'll try again. She looked at the sandwiches and then shook her head. No, she thought. I just can't. She reached for a fresh bottle of water and drank, her eyes on the door and then back to Graeme. She needed to get him out of there but how?

Her attention was caught as Graeme's head started to toss from side to side and he began mumbling. What is he talking about, she wondered, catching the odd word about the MacKay building?

———

What did he find there he shouldn't have? She reached for some napkins, dampening them to wipe down his face, finding it warm under her hand.

This went on for days. The same routine. Sue was tired, tired of being locked up, tired of not being able to move freely, tired of the same timing of their food being brought in. She had stopped counting the days, growing more weary as each hour went by.

She didn't know what day it was that they were moved from there. She stumbled up the steps, watching closely as Graeme was dragged up them, his feet not working as they should, before they were once more shoved into the van and taken away. She tried to make out where they were going but couldn't. The movement of the van was too jarring and it just didn't make sense the route they were taking. She sat close to Graeme, an arm around him to steady him, a wish in her heart that she was at home. God, are You even there right now?

Graeme stirred as the van stopped, shaking his head and then groaning.

"Why did I do that? It hurts." He heard movement beside him and squinted in the darkness.

"Of course it does. You were hit over the head with a bat and haven't had any medical treatment. What did you expect when you shook it?" There was a trace of amusement in the feminine voice he heard.

"Who are you? And where are we? It's dark"

"I'm Sue. We've been abducted, just why I have no idea. And we are once more in the van. You were

—

knocked out the last time we were taken out of it. Don't try it again. It would likely kill you." Sue's voice was stern as she stared at the door, waiting for it to open. When it didn't, she rose to her feet and walked quietly towards it, an ear pressed to the metal to listen. She heard the sound of a vehicle driving away and then shook with fear.

"Graeme? I think they just drove off and left us." Sue banged at the door and then shoved at it, trying to open it.

Graeme rose on shaky legs and running his hand along the side of the van walked towards her.

"Can't get it open?" He heard a sound of frustration from her. "Here, let me. There is sometimes a release inside the van, just in case." He felt along the door and then pulled on a lever. "And there is. Watch yourself." He shoved upwards on the door, watching as daylight, or dusk, rather, he thought, appeared.

Sue was out of the van and on the ground, her eyes searching. "I don't see anyone. Come on, Graeme. Move it."

He carefully jumped down, regretting it as his head pounded with pain, pain that caused him to waver and his eyes to shut. Sue sighed, reaching for his arm.

"This way, Graeme. I have a good idea where we are. Let's move. Graeme?" She stood for a moment, studying his face before she pulled him with her. "This way."

He tightened his grip on her hand. "Sue, is it?" When she nodded, her eyes tracing his face for a moment, he continued. "Why were we taken? Do you know?"

She shook her head, even as she kept them moving forward. "I don't. I think they were after you, but I happened to be there. You took me down in the park near my work and then they were there before we could escape."

"Park? Near your work? What exactly do you do?"

Sue stopped for a moment, just to let him catch his breath. "I'm a police detective. And you are a painter. I could see them going after me. But you? What did you go and do?"

Graeme shrugged, finding the world fading a bit around his line of sight. "I don't know. I can't remember." He squinted once more as he stared down the street. "Where are we heading?"

"There's a little convenience store just down the road. It should be open still. I can get us help there."

Graeme's hand suddenly tightened on hers and he pulled her away from the sidewalk to cover. Sue glared at him and then searched the street, before she was pulling him back towards it, waving down the oncoming car.

Graeme protested but sank gratefully down onto the seat of the patrol car, even as Sue was rapidly describing his condition and asking, no, demanding he thought, that he be taken to the hospital.

—

27

Frankie stared at her. "Where did you come from, Sue?"

"I have no idea, but there is a van back there you need to take to our facilities." Her faced turned to watch Graeme, not seeing the speculative glance she was given. "And keep it off the air that you have us. Call Caleb on his cell and have him meet us."

Chapter 5

Caleb's runners sent up squeaking sounds as he walked across the tiled floor in the Emergency Room. He frowning, thinking to himself that he needed to buy some new ones before he stopped in front of Frankie.

"Frankie? You called and asked me to meet you here. Why?" Caleb's face was stern but compassion was in his eyes.

"Caleb?" Frankie looked around before he pointed to the outside doors. "Let's talk outside for a moment."

"What about?" Caleb paused just outside the door, seeing the agitation in Frankie.

"I have Sue and Graeme here, getting looked at."

Caleb spun to stare back at the door. "Sue? How?"

Frankie shrugged, still not sure himself what had happened. "I found them walking down the sidewalk near the old MacKay building. By themselves. Sue said there was a van behind them she wanted us to look at. It was gone by the time I had someone there."

"Gone? This sounds as if it's a set up. Who do we have with them?"

"Grace's with Sue. Eddie was around and he's with Graeme."

Caleb turned to walk back through the doors. "How are they?"

"Sue's okay, I think. Dehydrated and hungry. She had refused to eat, she said. Graeme was unconscious for much of the time. Sue said he took a hard blow to his head from a bat. She's tried to treat him as much as she could."

Caleb nodded, his thoughts racing. "We need to keep it quiet that they're here, I would suspect. This sounds like they were just let go. We know they'll be watched." He gave a grim smile. "Sue will not like this, not at all."

"No, she won't. She'll be wanting to work it and she can't. How do we stop her?"

Caleb shrugged, his eyes on his detective as she walked towards him. "Sue?"

"Caleb? Frankie called you, I suppose. Grace's taken my statement."

"That's good. Now, you're staying here tonight." At her protect, his hand went up. "No, you're staying here. You've been through trauma. Tonight, you are a victim, not the detective." He grinned at the look that crossed her face.

She looked around, seeing Grace standing near her, a puzzled look on her face. "Where is Graeme?"

"Graeme is right behind you."

Sue spun at his voice. "Graeme, you need to be laying down. You have a concussion."

He carefully shook his head, his hand reaching for hers and pulling her towards him. "No. I don't have to. The physician says I just need to be careful how I move and take the pain medications as I need to."

She snorted, causing the other three to look at her. "Like you will? I tried that with you, remember?"

"You did? I don't remember, but I gather I refused them. I don't do medications. Never have. Now, where are we off to? I don't suppose we'll be allowed to go home."

"And why not?"

"The victims are never allowed to. They are always put into protective custody." He grinned at her frown as she shook her head. "That's how it works in movies, isn't it?" He looked past her as Frankie couldn't quite hide his snicker. "Care to introduce me?"

Sue stared down at their linked hands, not wanting to remove hers, feeling safe and cherished for some reason, before she looked back up at him.

"Sure. The one behind me? That's Caleb Logan, our police chief. Beside him is Frankie Brennan, a fellow detective. Behind you is Grace, one of our other detectives. Eddie Brown was with you. Now, can we go somewhere?"

Frankie looked past her at Eddie, who nodded.

Eddie spoke, his arm coming around Sue. "I'll take you to Peg, Sue. Both of you. She'll find clothes for you to change into. We can't let you go to your own placed right at the moment. In fact, Grace here will go shopping for you both."

Grace nodded. "I can do that. Graeme, let me know your sizes and preferences for colours. Sue, I think I know you well enough." Sue and Grace exchanged glances before Sue nodded.

"Simply stuff, Grace. Just some plain jeans or leggings or sweaters. T-shirts or a sweatshirt." She stopped, blinking back tears for a moment. "I'm sorry. I don't have any money on me."

Grace reached to hug her. "It's okay, Sue. We can straighten up later. Let's get you out of here and settled. I have a feeling they're out there looking for you."

Sue snorted, causing the men with her to laugh, Graeme to stare at her in disbelief. "That's what they always do, right, Graeme? Just like in the movies?"

Graeme gave her a quick grin before he pulled her towards the door. "And on that note, I think they want us to move."

Chapter 6

An hour later, Sue gratefully sank down on the bed, feeling clean and more like herself. She twisted to stare at the closed door, before looking down at the pillow. Her head hit the pillow as she tumbled sideways, fatigue hitting her in a huge wave. She drew her feet up, curling her arms around herself.

I'll just lie here for a moment, she thought. I need to eat, to get something to drink, but I am so tired.

Sue didn't hear the tap at her door, before it cracked open. Peg Brown stood there, looking in at Sue before she turned to Eddie,

"She's asleep, Eddie. You'll have to talk to her later. Knowing Sue, she not likely slept much."

Eddie shook his head as he watched Peg reach for a blanket and cover the younger woman. "I doubt she did. We'll talk later, then."

Eddie paced back to the kitchen, his eyes on Graeme as the younger man struggled to stay awake, pain evident on his face. He reached to draw him to his feet, and hand on his shoulder, directed him to the living room couch.

Graeme sat, a brief nod given, before he too had laid down, his eyes closing against the headache he had. He didn't feel the blanket spread over him or hear the quiet conversation from the kitchen.

—

Frankie finally headed out, his eyes searching the surrounding neighbourhood. He could feel the eyes, the ones he and his wife, Deirdre, had felt as had so many of their friends. Keep these two safe, Lord. We don't know Graeme but I suspect we will get to over the next while. Sue? She's such a precious lady, dear to all of us. Protect her, Lord.

Caleb looked up from his desk as Frankie tapped at the door. "Frankie?"

"They're both asleep. Eddie's there. He'll talk to them when they awaken." He sank into a chair, exhausted. "We've had enough of this, Caleb. There have been too many friends this has happened to."

Caleb rubbed at his face as he stared down at the remaining paperwork on his desk. "Any news from the street?"

Frankie shook his head. He had gone to the sources he had accumulated when an undercover cop, but no one had heard anything. "They're quiet. That tells me that they know nothing, or that they're afraid to say."

"And your guess would be?"

"Fear. Whoever this is has to be high up in town or from outside of town with good contacts here." He sighed. "Haven't we done this already?"

Caleb gave a brief laugh. "We have, Frankie. That we have. You're not on call this weekend, are you?"

Frankie shook his head. "I'm not to be. Sue was, but who's covering for her?"

———

"Eddie picked it up. He said you and Deirdre had plans, and he didn't want you to cancel them."

"Deirdre cancelled them. She felt that Sue would need her, just to talk to. They have become close friends. So, I can cover for some of the weekend."

Caleb nodded, thinking through what Frankie had said. "We need to talk to Doug's wife, Darcy. Will she come on as a consultant for Sue? Do what she does best with her forensics psychology?"

Frankie started to laugh, causing Caleb to frown at him. He handed over a file. "Here, she already has. She started this the night Sue disappeared."

"She did? What did she come up with?"

"Not what you want to hear. She thinks there's a woman behind it." Frankie's eyes slid closed. "How do we find her? And why Sue?"

"I know. Sue just happened to be there, didn't she? But why was Graeme there? That's what I would like to know."

"That's got me puzzled as well. Eddie will find out for us. If he remembers." Frankie stood, heading for the door, his steps pausing for a moment before he shook his head and walked away.

Caleb slowly opened the folder he had been handed and began reading. She's good, is Darcy, he thought. Then his frown grew deeper as he read further. He paused, then reached for the folder, heading to make a copy for both Frankie and Eddie before he walked from the building, heading for a store

in town where he knew he would find Darcy.   He
needed to talk to her.

Chapter 7

Sue's eyes popped open, and she sat up abruptly, not sure as to where she was. She stared down at the clothes she was wearing, not recognizing them. She heard a tap at the door and froze, not sure if it was friend or foe. This was too nice a room to have been one they had been kept captive in.

"Sue?" Peg's voice caught her attention, and her eyes slid closed. She was with friends.

She was on her feet and hugging Peg before the older woman had completely entered the room.

"Peg? I'm at your place? How?"

Peg hugged her tightly and then stood back, her hands on Sue's arms. "Somehow you managed to get away. Eddie brought you here last night. You've slept for more than twelve hours." Her head tilted as she studied the whiteness and gauntness of Sue's face. "Knowing you, you didn't sleep or eat."

"No, I couldn't. I didn't know what they would have given me." She frowned. "There was a man there as well."

"Graeme."

Sue frowned. "Graeme? Do I know him?"

"Graeme McDiarmid. No, I don't think you did. I have met him at church. He's new to our town. But you, somehow, you ended up in the park near the station and were abducted with him. Come, before we talk anymore, Eddie wants to get your statement. He's already taken Graeme's."

"He was hurt that day. Peg? He shouldn't be here. He should be in the hospital."

Peg studied Sue for a moment, then nodded. I see the interest there, Lord, even if Sue hasn't yet.

Eddie watched Sue carefully, seeing just how on the edge she was. She didn't need this, Lord. She was just starting to recover from the shooting.

"Sue? Walk me through what happened. Graeme has already." His eyes watched Graeme as his head raised and he realized Sue was in the room.

Graeme frowned. Sue shouldn't be up, he thought. Then he mentally shook his head. He had no right to ask her to stop, to rest, although he would really like to have that right.

Sue finally sat back, her hand reaching for her cup of peppermint tea. "I think that's it, Eddie. I don't know of anything I can add." Her brow wrinkled for a moment. "No, there's nothing more." Her gaze rested on Graeme. "But I don't understand why you were there, in that park. It's not close to where you were working."

Graeme shook his head. "I had been heading for the library to do some research. I saw that van. It had been hanging around the house. I tried to hide, but you walked into the park. I couldn't let them hurt you."

—

Sue shook her head. "No, you couldn't. Instead, you just dropped me into whatever is going on with you. What is it about that building?"

"That's what I was trying to find out." He groaned. "I have to call the owner. He'll fire me, I just know it. We're on a deadline and I just lost a week to it."

Eddie shook his head. "I know Peter Mack. He's aware of what happened. He's more concerned that you are okay. He'll work with the deadline. He tells me it's not as important as you are."

"He did? Thanks, I guess."

Eddie laughed, even as he turned at voices in the hallway. "He's a good friend of ours. He understands. Caleb? What brings you by?"

Caleb dropped the folder he was carrying on the table and then reached to pour himself a mug of tea before sliding into a chair. His eyes went to Sue.

"Sue?"

"Caleb?" When he didn't speak, she shook her head, a small smile on her face. "I'm okay. Just tired and hungry."

"Of course you would be. You wouldn't have eaten or drank anything, just like you said. Eddie?"

"I have their signed statements, Caleb. Not that it moves the investigation forward very much."

"About what I expected." Caleb's eyes sought Sue's again, seeing the slight frown on her face. "Darcy's been working, Sue."

——

39

"She has? Of course, she has. What did she come up with?"

"First, we need to spend some time in prayer. Eddie?"

Graeme watched in amazement before all heads were bowed and Eddie prayed, followed by Caleb's voice. This was not what he had expected or been used to.

Chapter 8

Caleb flipped the folder open, deep in thought, before he closed it and looked up at first Graeme and then Sue.

"Sue? What are your thoughts?"

She shrugged. "I can't get a read on it yet. They asked us nothing, just left us there. It's like they were waiting for someone or something." She looked over at Graeme. "Graeme? Why would someone be after you?"

He shook his head. "I have no idea. I don't have any secrets in my life." He thought about her question and then shook his head again. "No, nothing I can think of. I'm not from here, so that's out."

"Not necessarily." Eddie spoke up. "We've had people who have gone through stuff in this town. And sometimes that stuff has followed them here."

Graeme blanched. "Are you saying I caused this?"

"No, we're not." Caleb watched him closely, his eyes narrowing.

Sue finally reached for the folder, surprised that Caleb's hand didn't move from it.

"Caleb?" She studied him, a frown on her face, seeing the concern and worry he didn't try to hide. "Is it that bad?"

He nodded. "It is. And Emma and Kat have been working. Adriel wants you to come stay with them."

Sue shook her head. "Not happening, Caleb. Not unless I have to."

He grinned. "Abe said you'd say just that. He's ready to have his team protect you and Graeme here."

Graeme had been watching the two, finally raising a hand to interrupt. "Who is Abe and why would he do that?"

"You have heard of Rebel's?"

"In a way. Why?"

"Abe Finlay runs a security company, more into training teams now. But he has offered his team of eight to protect you two if necessary. And before you ask, all eight of them had what we term as "adventures" just like you seem to be heading into. And a number of other friends of ours as well." He nodded at Eddie and Peg. "Abe is nephew to these two."

Graeme shook his head. "What did I walk into to? I took over Dad's business when he had to retire. Word got out what we were doing, and we talked it over and agreed I should take this job. It's not that far from my home." He frowned once more before he looked up at Sue. "Aren't you going to look at that?" He stabbed a finger towards the folder.

She stared at him for a moment, eyes narrowing, not seeing the glances shared between the others in the room. "What? This? Maybe. At some point. Of course, I could just go and talk with Darcy."

"Not without me, you're not." Graeme nodded at the paperwork. "Read it. I know you can't tell me what it says, but please, just reassure me it will help solve this."

They watched as Sue opened the folder, her eyes sliding closed for a moment, not sure if she wanted to read what Darcy had written.

Sue began to read, her brow furrowed as she did, before she sat back, her eyes focused on the far wall.

"Sue?" Caleb's voice brought her focus to him, watching as she shoved the folder over to Eddie. "Talk to me."

"How does she do this? I can never figure it out, how they can profile someone they have never met."

"I can't explain it. You know what she did when she and Doug had that episode. She was bang on with her work." Eddie looked up from the notes. "And I would safely say she is once more." He turned to Graeme, seeing the puzzlement on his face. "Doug Foster is one of our ETF leaders. Darcy is his wife. I am not sure if you've met them at church or not. Darcy used to work as a forensic psychologist and did profiles of suspects for police departments. That's what she has done here. Without being asked. That's how she is. She and Sue are friends."

Caleb groaned, bringing all eyes to him. "Graeme, did you happen to have a friend by the name of Murphy O'Brien?"

—

"I used to. I haven't seen or heard from him since college." His gaze went to Sue. "You're Sue!"

"Of course, I am. Wait. Gray? You're the one who wanted to be an artist? I knew you were familiar."

"That would be me. I headed home after college. Dad got sick and needed me." He frowned. "You had a friend, Elle. Do you know where she is?" He looked around as they began to laugh. "What did I say?"

"Adriel or Elle as I called her lives here. In fact, she and Murphy are married."

"They are? Oh, I'll have to track them down." More laughter had him staring at Sue. "Now, what did I say?"

"Murphy is one of Abe's security team. You know, the ones we don't want brought in. Although Ian would likely fly us somewhere safe. He's always threatening that." Sue laughed at the look on Graeme's face. "Don't worry, Gray. I'll make sure you get introduced to them all." She looked back at Eddie. "Now, Eddie? Where do we go?"

"She's good, isn't she?"

"That she is. She read it well for us that time we had the trouble with that police chief." Caleb tapped at the folder. "I think she has this time as well."

"I'm sure she has. How do we work this?"

"You don't, Sue." His hand up, Caleb just shook his head. "You can't. Not officially. You're involved in it. Now, if you were to hang around with Graeme here, and go through the MacKay home and do some research on your own time, I couldn't stop you."

———

44

Sue stood for a moment in the doorway of her home. She had insisted she come back there. She was afraid, terrified, she thought, over what had happened. Sneaking a look behind her, Sue finally entered her home, eyes narrowing as she searched. No, she thought, no one had been in there.

Graeme hesitated at the door, not sure if he was to follow her or not. He finally sighed, stepping in and closing the door gently behind him.

"Graeme? Come on in and to the kitchen." Sue's voice was tired. She knew Peg had not wanted her to come home yet, but she couldn't stay. Something was driving her to move forward, to find who it was, and that would be a task. She knew that only too well.

He walked forward, his eyes roaming her home, liking what he saw. The soft yellows of the walls with the off-white wainscoting was a nice touch, he thought. Not how she had described the home she wanted. He felt something brush against his leg and stopped, eyes searching the floor before he smiled and reached for the small gray tabby kitten who sat, face turned up to his. She cuddled down in his arms as he stroked her before heading for the kitchen.

"Sit, Gray. We need to talk." Sue turned from the counter and pointed to a chair at the cream wood table.

—

"Thanks, Sue." Graeme gave a quick grin. "Still drinking that herbal stuff?"

She laughed. "I still am." She paused, her hands stilling on the coffee pot she had reached for. "Murphy asked me that not long ago."

"Murphy? ? Of course he would. You say he's in the area?"

Sue looked down at him as she set the mug of coffee in front of him. "He is. He went into the security business with Abe. You remember Abe Finlay?"

"I do, now that I think about. So much has happened in the last ten years or so, Sue. So much water under the bridge." He watched as she slid a plate of muffins onto the table with a selection of jams. "We need to catch up, but this is not how I ever expected meeting you again. I never thought of you as being a police officer."

She shrugged as she raised her cup of tea to sip through. "That was my goal all along, I think, Gray. I have had the opportunity to rise quickly in this force. We have a young police chief, but he's good. He's so in touch with his officers and staff. He cares and it shows."

"It does. I could see that." Graeme's eyes were on his hands as he wrapped them around his mug. "How are you really doing, Sue? Something happened in the recent past, didn't it?"

She stilled once more, her eyes on her cup before she raised them to his, seeing the caring and

—

compassion she had always felt from him. "It did. I was shot a few months ago. I almost didn't make it. My friends tell me God isn't done with me yet."

"But you never believed, Sue. Not that I was aware of. You always avoided that talk if you could." He watched as her eyes slid closed and a single tear tracked down her cheek.

Sue jumped as she felt Graeme's finger on her cheek, wiping away her tear. She had never cried in front of him, so why now. She heard his chair move and then his arms around her, hugging her, trying to comfort her. Then, she heard his whispered prayer for her, for comfort, for peace, for healing.

Graeme finally sat back, concern on his face, before his head turned as the doorbell rang. His hand kept Sue in her chair as he rose and headed for the front door. He opened, watching as the couple around his age turned back to face him.

Murphy O'Brien stared at the man in front of him. "Graeme? Graeme McDiarmid? What? You're here?"

"Murphy O'Brien. I am and so are you." Graeme reached to shake Murphy's hand, standing aside as Murphy drew the woman with him forward. "And Elle."

"Gray?" Adriel moved to hug him. "I am so glad to see you. How are you involved in this?" She waved her hands. "No, let me guess. You're the man that went missing with Sue?"

———

48

"That would be me. Sue's in the kitchen." His glance shot that way as a worried frown covered his face.

"I can see you took the brunt of whatever it was." Murphy's voice grew grim even as Adriel moved towards the kitchen.

"I did. Sue just happened to be there." Graeme's words came quickly as he brought Murphy up to date. "I have no idea why or who."

Murphy nodded. "Let's talk at some point. Sue's still fragile from her shooting. We're afraid this will set her back." He watched as Graeme shook his head. "You don't think it will."

"No, I don't. Sue was a good friend. I would like to think she still is. She has a way of appearing fragile and needing help, but she has a well of determination and courage deep inside her that she draws from. I have seen it in the past." He paused, his eyes closing. "Now, there's someone we need to look at. He hated both of us."

"Let me have his name and I'll get Emma to look it up."

"Emma?" Graeme frowned.

"You remember Emma Donovan? She's married to Abe. They have quite a story to tell. Anyway, she's set up a business of tracking people and is so good at that. She'll search him through."

"She always had a mindset for that. I'm glad she's using it." Graeme paused for a moment, before

———

he shook his head, turning to walk back to the kitchen, stopping as he heard Adriel and Sue talking.

Murphy stared at him, and then moved around him to greet Sue, reaching for the coffee pot to fill mugs for both Adriel and himself, refilling Graeme's

"Now what, Sue?" His voice was gentle as he hugged his friend, before sitting. "How do we help you?"

She shrugged, her eyes on Graeme. "I don't know. For now, Caleb wants me off work. I go back mid-week, he said, under orders that I can't officially research this."

"But I know you and so does he. You won't stay away from it." Adriel reached for her friend's hand, a prayer rising in her heart. "Has Darcy weighed in?"

Sue laughed, the laughter lighting up her face. "She has already. I've seen it. She thinks a woman is the one behind it."

Adriel exchanged a glance with Murphy, her eyes resting on Graeme for a moment. "That makes sense, Sue. In a bizarre way. We've seen it too many times. Too many of our friends have gone through something."

Graeme choked on his coffee. "Friends? Like in how many?"

"A dozen or more I would think. Likely closer to two dozen. Not just friends from here." Murphy sought Sue's eyes, watching as she nodded. "Even Caleb's family has been affected. Two of her cousins were involved in stuff as we call it."

Graeme stared at them before he shook his head. "That's not true. It can't be. It sounds like a movie or television serial."

The three with him laughed.

"It did. Now, where do we go from here?" Sue rose, heading for her office, returning with her laptop and pads of paper and pens.

Chapter 10

Sue finally shut the door after the three, leaning back against it as she thought through what they had talked about. She was fatigued, bone weary, she decided, reaching to pick up the kitten who was trying to crawl up her leg. She cuddled her close even as she moved through to shut drapes, turn out lights, make sure the doors were locked and the security system set.

She sighed as she sank down onto her bed, not even with enough energy to clean up and change for bed. Her head hit the pillow as she pulled blankets around her, asleep before she was even aware that she was in bed.

Graeme paced the small camper that he had brought in and set up at the MacKay house, his thoughts on the discussions he had been part of. He shook his head, amazed that he had connected with Sue again. He had missed her, he realized, and her refreshing outlook on life.

He frowned as he stood at the counter, his hand on the kettle. Now, what was that thought he had just had? He tapped his fingers lightly on the countertop before he turned, a groan rising from him. He hurried to his desk, pulling out the paperwork he had accumulated, a hand rubbing at his forehead and the headache he had.

He sat, a cup of tea in front of him, not even realizing what he had made, as he sorted through the

---

papers and photos, finally stopping at one, a finger tracing the woodwork. This is why, isn't it, Lord? There's something in there, something hidden. Either someone is afraid I will find it or else they want me to. I don't get which. Not yet.

He thought back to the conversation with Caleb. Now, there's a man who doesn't overlook anything. I need to talk to him about this, but I also have to talk to Sue. He reached for his phone and then saw the time. No, it's way too early in the morning. He rose, stretched, shuffled the papers back together and then opened the safe he had installed in the camper, shutting and locking it before heading for his own bed. He stretched out, sighing with relief, his eyes closing as he prayed, prayed for understanding, for wisdom, for peace for his friend. He knew she was still fighting something. And he prayed that she would let him in and let him help her.

Graeme rose the next morning, finding he was still stiff but moving better than he had been. He frowned as he stared at himself in the mirror before he shrugged, heading for the kitchen and his morning coffee. An hour later, he stood in the house he was painting, searching for something that felt off but not seeing it. He reached for his paint, brushes, and rollers and walked up the stairs to the second floor, searching once more for something off and not seeing it.

Three hours later, he heard a knock at the door and glanced at his watch. No one was to be here. He covered the tray of paint, rolled his brush and roller into plastic and headed down the stairs. Standing at the open door, he watched as Frankie turned to him.

—

53

"Graeme? How are you?"

He shrugged. "I have no idea how I am to feel. I've never been through this before." His words had a bite to him that caused Frankie to grin and then hold up the coffees in his hand.

"Ready for a break?"

Graeme nodded, and pointed to the porch. "We can sit out here, if you like. This is where I sit to refresh myself."

Frankie nodded even as he sat, his eyes wandering the area, liking what he saw. Sipping at his coffee, he waited for Graeme to speak.

Graeme waited as well. He was in no hurry, he decided. Let Frankie speak first.

Frankie grinned. "Not biting, I see." He laughed as Graeme smiled and shook his head. "That's okay. I think you just need to rest for a moment. I just wanted to update you a bit. We did find the van. It was cleaned out and polished and washed thoroughly. Our techs could find nothing. Just curious, though. How did you know there was a lever inside?"

The younger man shrugged, running a hand through his hair. "I had a friend who worked for the company that serviced them. He told me about them, showed me in fact. It was a similar style van. I was just praying when I searched that it had the lever."

"And it did. Does Sue know this isn't always the case?"

Graeme shrugged. "I have no idea. We didn't talk about that." He frowned at Frankie. "But that's not why you're here."

"No, it isn't. We received a letter about you, Graeme. I have a copy here that I want to show you. Just let me preface it by saying I have talked to Murphy and Adriel, Abe and Emma, Sue. They all tell me you are an honourable man, not given to tricks or violence."

"I'm not. Did you say Abe and Emma? They live here?" He shook his head. "I knew Abe did. Just not that Emma did. No, wait. They told me that, didn't they? I think I'm confused. I had too much thrown at me yesterday when I wasn't thinking too clearly."

"That you did." Frankie agreed with him, knowing that he was going to throw even more at him. "I'll leave this for you. Call me when you read it and think it over. I need to let you get back to work." Rising, he dropped the folder on the chair he had been sitting in and walked away, not saying anything more.

Graeme stared after him and then at the folder, before he too rose, picking it up and heading for his camper, locking it into his safe. He glanced at the time. No, he thought, I don't feel like eating lunch today. He walked away, locking his camper, and heading back to his painting.

Five hours later, he stood in his camper, showered, shaved, and knowing he needed to eat. But he wanted to see Sue. That drove him from his home and to his truck, heading for a local restaurant to pick up a meal, and then to Sue's. He didn't know what she

—

liked anymore or even if she had already eaten. He just needed to see her, to talk to her, to hear her laugh. He realized how much he had missed her.

Sue looked up from her desk as she heard the doorbell and sighed. There had been a number of friends through or calling her today. She had finally muted her phone, ignored the doorbell, and worked away on her investigation. She rose, rubbing at her lower back, before she paced through on bare feet to stare out the door. He just had to come back, now didn't he, Lord? What am I to do with him? And he has food. She realized she hadn't eaten that day and was ravenous.

Chapter 11

Turning as Sue spoke, Graeme studied her face, realizing that she was just like she had been the day before. He stepped through the door, closing it behind him, heading for the kitchen to set down the food before he turned, sweeping her into a hug, feeling her hug him back. I've come home, he thought, wondering where that had come from. They were friends, just reuniting.

Sue finally stood back, her eyes assessing Graeme before she pointed to the food.

"What do you have there, Gray?"

"I took a chance that you hadn't eaten and picked up what you used to like. Cheeseburger with the works, fries, soft drink."

"You didn't, did you? I've been craving one, just haven't taken the time to get one. Sit." Sue reached to pull the food out. "And you got your favourite as well. Nice."

They talked quietly as they ate, Sue finally gathering up their garbage and disposing of it, before she reached to pour Graeme his coffee and herself the tea she enjoyed.

"It's a nice night. Let's sit out back."

He followed her, watching as she clicked out most of the inside lights before sinking down on a swing on her back deck. He sat beside her, the folder he had brought balancing on his knee.

"What do you have there, Graeme?" Sue finally spoke, her eyes on his face.

"Frankie was by the worksite today. He left this. I haven't looked at it. But he seemed to think I needed to." He looked up at Sue. "Before I do, or rather we do, we need to pray, Sue. I feel like I am being sucked into the vortex of a tornado, with no chance of escape or survival."

"I know that feeling. I'm there, right with you." She poked at the folder. "So what did Frankie leave you?"

"A letter, he said. I have not read it. I locked it away while I was at work." He turned to her, reaching for a hand. "We need to pray, Sue. Right now, before we look at this."

She nodded. "Go ahead. Please?"

Graeme nodded, his eyes on her averted face, before he sighed and then prayed. He hesitated when he was finished, looking out across her backyard, seeing the sun setting, hearing the sounds of twilight and night starting as the sounds of sunset and day faded. It was his favourite time of night, he thought.

He felt her reach for the folder, a question of her face that he nodded to in answer, and then she opened the folder.

Sue drew in her breath. This is brutal, she thought. How and what did Graeme get involved in?

—

"Sue? I don't like the look on your face." He reached for the folder, gently taking it from her before his eyes dropped, and a grave look crossed his face. "This is what you deal with all the time?"

She sighed. "It is. I have seen way worse, but this is brutal. What are you involved in, Graeme?"

He shrugged. "I have no idea. I was just contacted to paint the house. I have no idea of its history. I found pictures online from what it should look like, given the era it's from, but no pictures or history of it." He stopped talking, his eyes shooting to hers. "And I should have, given that it's a heritage house."

"You should have. And suddenly I don't know that I ever heard of it being designated as that. We'll look into that. For now. What are your thoughts on the letter?"

His eyes dropped and he re-read it, finally reading it out loud.

"McDiarmid

"You have become involved in something that is not your affair. Yesterday was a warning. Continue to work here, and your life is forfeit. As is your lady's.

"You have been warned."

"I have no idea who would be doing this." Graeme sat back after throwing the folder onto the table beside him. "How well do you know the homeowner?"

"I don't know him at all, but I have asked Emma to look into him." At his glance, she sighed. "This has

---

to stay between us. You have heard of Tracker's?
That's Emma. It's her story to tell, but suffice it to say,
she is brilliant."

"She always was. She thought way outside of
the box. I know our professors were scared of what
she'd say next or what she'd come up with."

Sue nodded, content finally just to sit. She felt
Graeme's arm around her, drawing her close, and
suddenly once more felt safe and at peace. Lord,
what's going on here? I don't know if I can do this
right now.

Chapter 12

Caleb turned from the counter in the break room the next morning, hearing Sue's voice, and sighed. She's not to be in here yet. He walked to the doorway, where he stood, watching as she spoke with Eddie, her eyes on him, before she walked towards him.

"Sue? You're not due in yet." Caleb's voice, though kindly, was stern.

"I know. I talked to Graeme last night. He showed me the letter." She held up a hand. "As a friend, Caleb, and as one who is involved deeply in this. We had a question. How much have you looked into the house and the owner?"

Caleb nodded, knowing Sue was digging into it on her own. "We're looking into that. I am not sure yet where that investigation stands. But, Sue, you need to follow orders. I need you to come back rested and well enough to work on your cases."

She snorted, bringing a grin to his face. "I can come back now, Caleb. I can't sit around. You know that. You know how that affects me."

"I do, so I'm going to overlook this. But you can't stay all day, not working the hours you have been. Pace yourself. I'll hold you to that."

"Thank you, Caleb." Sue paused deep in thought before she looked up at Caleb, her face going white. "I think I have a case that's connected." She spun, almost

—

on a run for her office, Caleb staring after her before he followed.

"Just what do you mean, Sue?"

She searched through the pile of folders on her desk, pulling one. "This one. The Whittaker case. He's connected to the MacKay family, way back. I've been researching it, trying to get a sense of why he was killed."

"And now you think you do?" Caleb sighed even as he reached for the folder. "Sue, is this why? It's not just Graeme then. It's you, too. How do I keep you safe?"

Sue shrugged, her eyes already on her work, her mind drifting to that. "I have no idea, Caleb. And no, I will not go hide out at Abe's."

Caleb shook his head as he walked away. He and Abe had spoken of that, knowing it might well come to putting the two away. He almost said couple, his steps slowing as he pictured them from a couple of days before. Yes, Lord, I can see them as a couple.

Sue finally raised her head from her paperwork, setting the phone back on its base, before she shuffled through the folders, finding the one she wanted. There had to be a connection between the MacKay house and this one, but I'm not seeing it. She frowned as she rose and walked towards the break room, not seeing Eddie behind. Eddie watched closely even as he followed her, needing to talk with her, but not sure how to approach her.

"Sue?"

She spun, a hand coming to her throat. "Eddie. I didn't hear you."

"No, you didn't. You were lost in thought. Care to share?" He reached for the coffee carafe and frowned, then dumped the contents to make fresh.

Sue stared at him before she nodded. "I do. What do you know of the MacKay house?"

"I know of it. It's been standing empty for a number of years until it was bought last year. I heard rumours that the historical society was trying to have it deemed historical, but now that I think of it, I don't think it ever was." His eyes on Sue's face, he caught the slight frown that passed over her face. "This is what it's about? What happened to you and Graeme?"

She nodded. "I think so, but I'm not sure. I didn't remember hearing that had passed through the city council. I have searched and don't see any designation of that. So, why would Graeme be told that?" She looked around as Frankie paused in the doorway, moving towards them. "Frankie?"

"Sue? Did Graeme catch up with you last night?"

"He did. It shook him, Frankie. I don't know that I've seen that from him before." Sue began to pace, stopping in front of Eddie, searching his face and seeing his nod. "You expected that, didn't you, Eddie? Of course, you would. That's what always happens, isn't it?"

Eddie grinned at her. "As you say, Sue, it always does." He reached for the folder he had in his hand.

"Now, I need to talk to you. Not as detective to detective. As detective to victim. Can you do that for me?"

She finally nodded, walking away and heading for his office, leaving the two men to watch her.

"How is she really doing, Eddie?" Frankie was concerned for his friend.

"That, I don't know. She hides her emotions and feelings well. She has learned that. There is something in her past that has driven her to that." He sighed, heading for the door. "Don't go poking into it, Frankie. Let her talk to us."

Sue watched as Eddie sank into a chair beside her rather than behind his desk. He's wearing out, she thought. He needs to take some time, take a vacation, but he won't. Not while this is going on. He'll work until he collapses if this isn't solved soon. He's been through so much in the last few years, what with everyone who has had what we term as "adventures". Lord, bless my friend. Give him healing.

Chapter 13

Studying Sue for a moment, Eddie sighed. This is getting old, Lord. I'm tired. I'm worn out. I need to solve this and then decide what I want to do. I need to talk to Ben Johnson but how?

"Sue, this is difficult. We have worked so many cases together. I never thought I would be working one where you were the victim."

"I know. I don't like it." She glared at him as he laughed. "I know. Everyone has said that at some time or other. What can you tell me?"

"I know you're poking into it on your own time. Caleb has expected that. You need to keep us up to date on what you're finding, let us verify it. We can't have a case thrown out of court."

"I get that, Eddie. But I just can't not do anything."

"We know that as well, Sue. Now, that building. It has never been declared historical. I spoke with the historical society. They had approached the city and then backed away. I am afraid for Graeme. He's been given false information and I need to track down where that originated."

"I think with the homeowner." She sat back, her eyes on the floor. "How did they reach out to him? Did you talk to him about that?"

—

"Not yet, but we intend to. Leave that for now. The van? It was clean. Did you know Graeme has a friend who services those and showed him one time how to find the door latch?"

She shook her head. "I wasn't aware of that, but that doesn't surprise me. He was always into things like that, having to know how something worked and wasn't satisfied until he did." Her head went back. "What did he go and get involved in, Eddie? I fear for his life. After that letter he showed me, it's only a matter of time until things escalate."

"That is true. I would suspect it to. It always does." Eddie studied her more closely. "You need to watch yourself, Sue. What is in your background that would tie you to this building or to Graeme?"

She shrugged. "Nothing that I am aware of. You know me, Eddie. We've talked. This is not my hometown but it is my town. I can't see anything in my past that would connect me to here."

Eddie nodded again, his eyes on the doorway as Frankie hesitated and then moved on. "Are you sure?"

Sue stared at him for a moment, then shrugged. "Not that I am aware of. Dad and Mom don't come here, I always go there. Mom can't travel well, given her health issues now. I don't have anything in my past, not that I am aware of. The only connection I have with Graeme is college and even then it was through church that we connected. We didn't share classes or anything like that."

Eddie was watching her closely. "Just your church? Tell me about that."

———

She stared at him, her mind going back to the church she had attended. "It was a larger church, larger than here. We didn't have a lot of choice in where we attended. It wasn't the greatest for friendliness. The pastor saw to that." She frowned. "I always wondered how he got to be a pastor. He just didn't fit the role."

Eddie nodded. "Let me have his name and the names of anyone else you would like us to look at. Emma and Jace have asked."

She nodded. "I can do that. I'll work on that tonight. Graeme can likely give us names as could Murphy, Adriel, Emma, Abe."

Eddie watched her face, seeing the fatigue in it. "You need to go home, Sue. Leave this for the night. Pick it up tomorrow." He stood, his eyes thoughtful. "Watch yourself. I don't have to tell you that, you already know what to watch for. But it won't matter that you're a police officer. They've already proven that."

"And that's what I don't get. Why take me? Why just leave us like that? Did they know Graeme could get us out of the van? I don't expect they thought we would be found so quickly."

Eddie just shook his head, waiting for Sue to tidy up her desk, and then walked her to her car. "Don't be out walking on your own. I know you like to run. Find a gym or somewhere you can use a treadmill or an indoor track where there are people around."

She stared at him before nodding. "I don't like that, Eddie, but I have to, don't I?"

Graeme followed Sue through her house in the early evening of that day, watching as she reached to pull a casserole from the oven, setting it on the table before she turned to him.

"You're here early, Graeme?"

"I am. I finished off one of the rooms and didn't want to start another one. This smells good." He grinned as she shook her finger at him.

"Sit. We'll eat, then talk." Sue slid onto a chair, watching as he reached for her hand, his head bowing as he prayed. She listened to his words, hearing not only a blessing on the food, but a plea for them to be kept safe and that the situation they found themselves in solved quickly.

Graeme pointed to her plate. "Eat, Sue. Then, we talk. I think you have found out information that you need to share with me."

"I do. And I think you have done the same." She stared down at her plate, her fork moving through her food, before she began to eat. "This is hard, you know? Being on this side of an investigation."

"I am sure it is." Graeme ate in silence for a few minutes before he laid down his fork. "You're not eating, Sue."

"No, I'm not. I don't have an appetite tonight." She looked up at him. "I used to go to church with you every once in a while. Eddie asked me about that. I told him that was where we usually connected, that we didn't have classes together."

"And he's asked for names?"

"He did. I said we'd get him some."

Graeme nodded, rising and heading for the counter where he picked up the pad of paper and pens. He seated himself, tearing off some paper and handing the rest to Sue.

"Eat as you write, Sue. You know you can do that. At least, you used to." He grinned as she made a face at him, before her fork was back in her hand and she was eating, lost in thought.

They compared lists, combining them, before Sue sat back, her eyes on her friend.

"Graeme, what did we just do? Did we accuse innocent people?"

Graeme shook his head. "Not at all. What we have done is what Eddie asked. He asked for a list of people we both knew. This is it." He tapped his finger on the paper. "But what about your past, your younger years?"

Sue shrugged. "I don't recall anyone from them. How about you?"

He shook his head. "Not on my part. I'll need to talk to Dad, and see what he has to say. It may be related to someone in our family, not us at all."

She groaned as he said that. "You have would have to, wouldn't you?" She stared down at her paper

———

70

and then began to add names. "Eddie will have my head, giving him so many."

"I'm sure he'll understand. This is what you do. Now, let me take a copy of that." His phone was out as he took a photo, his hand pausing for a moment as he studied the names. "I don't think we've missed anyone."

"I doubt it. I'll talk to Elle. You talk to Murphy. See what they come up with. They may have noticed something we didn't. And then there's Abe and Emma."

"Emma? The one who scared the professors?"

Sue grinned. "That Emma. I'll talk to her. In fact, I'll give her this list. She'll look into it for us." She missed the speculative look she was given before Graeme rose, reaching for their dishes, tidying up the kitchen for her.

"You didn't have to do that, Gray."

He shrugged. "I know. Now, can we set this aside and just wander your backyard? I like what I see."

Sue locked the door after him a few hours later, leaning back on it, a smile on her face. Graeme had always made her feel special and cherished. Lord? Did You do this? Did You bring him back into my life?

She didn't see the car parked across from her in the empty driveway of a neighbour's house, the two men in it watching closely as Graeme drove away, followed by another car, or their attention turn back to her home.

Chapter 15

Frankie's attention was on the paperwork Eddie had handed him, before his eyes raised to see Sue standing beside him, a frown on her face.

"Frankie? That investigation you started a week ago? The one into the break-in at the historical society building? Where does it stand?"

Frankie watched her closely before he spoke. "We're still looking into it. The security guard that was injured hasn't been able to help much. He didn't see who attacked him." He paused, a frown on his own face. "That has to be one of the oddest investigations I've undertaken. Nothing was taken. Nothing was added. There is nothing to suggest why or what they were after."

"I can tell you what they were after. They were looking for anything on the MacKay house." With that, she turned and walked away.

Eddie shook his head. "She's likely right, Frankie."

Frankie sighed. "I know she is. I'm heading back there. I had intended to anyway today." He walked away, leaving Eddie staring after him before he shook his head, his attention going back to the list of names Sue had handed him. He read through it as he headed for his own office, greeting his fellow officers as he did so. A name stopped him in his tracks and his

—

eyes slid closed before he spun and headed for Caleb's office.

"Caleb? Got a moment?"

Caleb looked around from his fax machine and pointed to a chair. "I just need to finish this. What do you have?"

"Sue and Graeme were busy last night. She handed us a list of names. There's one here. We've looked into it before."

"And that name would be?" Caleb sat, his eyes on his friend.

"Gordon Ames."

Caleb nodded. "He's been a suspect in so many investigations. We have never been able to prove anything or catch him. Did she indicate how they knew him?"

"From the church they went to. I remember hearing that he had been in the leadership there, moved here, and tried to get into leadership in our church."

"And he has never been able to. Our people seem to be able to read him." Caleb rubbed at the back of his neck, fear for Sue running through him. "Run with it, Eddie. See what you come up with. Take it to Emma as well."

"I think Sue said they had passed the list on to her already." Eddie stood, his eyes on Caleb. "You know she's not going to sit back, not at all."

"No, I don't expect her to. But just make sure she passes everything on to you, for you to investigate and verify."

Eddie nodded as he headed towards Sue's office, needing to speak with her. He watched as he saw her heading from the building, and shook his head. He would catch up with her later, he thought.

Sue stood in the doorway of the downtown building, her eyes narrowed as she watched the crime scene techs. She sighed to herself, looking at her watch. Her day just grew in hours, knowing she wouldn't be meeting with Graeme any time soon. She sent him a quick text, her attention moving to the patrol officer heading her way.

She frowned as he spoke, before turning to study the building.

"You're sure it's his?"

"We are. It looks as if Ames has been buying up buildings and has been for a few months." He looked around as well, his eyes on the onlookers. "Somehow, Sue, I think our vandals are here somewhere."

"I am sure they are. Pull security video, whatever you need. You have this down to a science by now, Leroy."

He laughed. "That I do. Take care, Sue."

Sue finally stood at her desk, a folder open in her hands as she read the report from the responding officers. Something was off, she thought, but what. She sighed, dropping the closed folder to her desk. She would look at it afresh in the morning, she thought, and talk to the techs.

Graeme rose from her front steps as she approached, his head tilted as he watched her. She's tired in so many ways, Lord. How do I help her?"

"Graeme?" Her face lit up as she saw him. "You're here?"

"I am. Looking for a friend to share a meal with me. You're exhausted."

She nodded, unlocking the door, and hearing him enter behind her, the sound of his shoes hitting the mat in her ear. "I am. It's been a busy day." She looked around as his hand on her arm stopped her.

"Go, get changed, sweetheart. I'll look for some food for us. You have a grill?"

"I do. There is chicken in the fridge or meat patties in the freezer. Fresh veggies. Pull out what you want."

Sue's steps felt heavy as she climbed the stairs, her hand running along the railing, fatigue drawing her down. She shook her head, knowing that she needed to talk to Graeme, just not sure how to.

Graeme finally sat back from his meal, his hand reaching for Sue's. "Let's walk your yard. Then we talk." His finger on her mouth kept her silent before she nodded, rising, her hand in his.

Thirty minutes later, she sank into her swing, Graeme at her side. "It was a busy day, Graeme. How was yours?"

He smiled as he shrugged. "I was able to get another room done. The upstairs is almost finished. Then I move to the main floor." His head tilted as he watched her. "You're upset."

"I am, and I can't go into details. It's about an investigation. It frustrates me." She turned to watch his face. "Graeme, what did you do?"

He shrugged. "I talked to Dad last night. We're puzzled as to why our company was chosen. We have never worked in Riverville before, so why now?"

"I think you were chosen for a reason. And I don't like the feeling that I'm getting. Who did your Dad anger?"

"I have no idea. Neither does Dad. He's talking to his friends, to see if they picked up on anything, but for now, that's a no go."

Sue blew out a breath. "It is a no go. I'm off tomorrow. I forgot that. I need to do something, to get away from here, but I'm not sure where I want to go."

"It's Saturday. I made a commitment to Dad that I would only work five days a week. So, where do you want to go?"

She stared at him, and then began to laugh. "This sounds like old times, Gray. How many times have you asked that?"

Chapter 16

A week later, Eddie was on a hunt. He needed to speak with Sue and just couldn't find her. Frankie watched before he approached him.

"Eddie?"

"Frankie! Have you seen Sue?"

Frankie shook his head. "She was here around lunchtime, but said she had an errand to run. She didn't say what it was."

"She's not in the building. And we just got word that someone has put a contract out on her. Grace is working that." Eddie turned, heading for the front of the building. "Rick, did you see Sue?"

"Not for a couple of hours. She headed out the front. She said she'd be back by 2, and that's long gone."

Eddie and Frankie exchanged looks before Frankie spoke up. "Did she say where she was heading?"

Rick shrugged. "Not really. She mentioned something about Mac's and then muttered something about a Graeme."

They left the building almost on a run, heading for Frankie's car. He slammed on the brakes as he neared the MacKay house, before their doors were

—

open and they were running for the building, finding Graeme standing on the porch, staring at them.

"What is it? You flew up here like you have been called for." Graeme searched their grim faces before he searched the street. "You're looking for Sue?"

"We are. Have you seen her today?" Eddie paused to catch his breath.

"No, I haven't. We're planning to meet at Mac's for dinner, but right now, I have no idea where she is." He paled as he saw the looks crossing their faces. "Give me a moment. I was just finishing putting my equipment away." He was away and back in less than five minutes. "Where are we searching?"

"Did you talk to her at all today, Graeme?" Eddie's voice was stern, hiding his emotions.

"No. We had talked late last night, planned to meet around six at Mac's." His eyes shifted between the two men. "What aren't you saying?"

"There's word a contract is out on her. We need to find her." Frankie searched the area as they drove around. "Where would she go?"

Graeme's brow furrowed. "Try the historical society, maybe?"

Eddie shifted in his seat to stare at him. "Why would you say that?"

The younger man shrugged. "Because she's been working through some stuff for one of her cases. She hasn't talked about it but said she needed to go there and do some research."

Eddie and Frankie shared a glance, Frankie giving a shrug as he headed that way. Their footsteps sounded hollow for a moment in the entryway before the two officers each took a floor, Graeme staying with Eddie.

They met back in the lobby, frowns in place, knowing Sue had been there earlier but had left.

Eddie's phone was out as he called her, reaching her voice mail. He nodded as Graeme waved his phone before a text was sent. Graeme heard the soft chime of a text message and looked down, a sigh of relief rising from him.

"She's okay, guys. She's at Mac's. She had to talk to him about her case, apparently." Graeme headed away from them, intent on finding Sue, leaving the two officers staring at one another before shaking their heads.

Sue looked up as Graeme slid onto the bench seat beside her, Frankie and Eddie across from her. She shook her head, not liking that they had tracked her down. God, are You even there? They tell me You are. I have felt You there, but this scares me. Help me, please, Lord?

"What the rush, fellows? I was heading back to the office." Her eyes searched the faces of the two men across from her before she turned to Graeme. "Gray, this is earlier than we said."

"I know it is, sweetheart, but these two gentlemen have spent time looking for you." He nodded at Eddie. "They need to talk to you. Not as a police officer. Not this time."

―――

She looked up at Eddie, and he could see the fear flickering in her eyes before she tamped it back down. This is not going to be easy, he thought. Lord, please lead here. She stared at her friends from the force, a shuttered look on her face as Frankie and Eddie exchanged glances, not quite sure how to approach Sue.

Graeme's hand rested on her shoulder as he leaned close to speak with her, his gaze directed out the window.

"Just listen, sweetheart. That's all they ask. That's what would you say to a victim."

Sue turned her face slightly to watch him, not seeing the looks on the others' faces. She sighed. This is what You meant, isn't it, Lord? I heard You speaking to me this morning. I didn't want to hear what You said, but You were warning me, weren't You?

"What did you want to talk to me about, guys, that was so urgent you couldn't wait until I got back?"

"Sue, you know how we work. You've become a target. We received word there's a contract out on you."

"Of course, there is." Her gaze shifted to Eddie. "What can you tell me?"

"There's not a lot of info yet, Sue. I'm trying to track it back, but whoever it is hints at the MacKay house. What is your connection to that, other than the obvious? We know you were researching it today."

She frowned. "I know. I can't understand that, Eddie. That place just keeps popping up and I don't know why."

"There has to be a connection, other than you knowing me, Sue." Graeme sat back, a frown now on his face. "We need to look into this deeper."

"We will. You two stay out of it." Frankie and Eddie walked away, leaving Graeme and Sue staring at each other, looking up as Mac slid their food in front of them.

Mac paused, his eyes on them. "Sue, watch yourself. I sense real danger approaching you."

She sighed. "I know, Mac. I just don't know why."

Chapter 18

Earphones on, her stride long and loose, Sue ran through her favourite park and along the hiking trails by the river, needing this outdoor time, this time to just let everything go. She watched closely as she moved through the area, waving at friends, weaving among the walkers and the mothers with their young children. She felt at peace, that Saturday, knowing that she had left her work at the office. Graeme had asked if they could do something that day, but she had shaken her head, a smile on her face at his frown. She needed a day, she told him, a day just for herself.

He had walked away from her and then walked right back, stating he was driving her to church on the Sunday and that he had plans for them. She had just shaken her head, a grin on her face, as he walked backwards away from her, an answering grin on his.

Her steps slowed as she neared her house, hearing her security system beeping and seeing a patrol car slowing to pull into her driveway. She shook her head at him, heading for the door, halting as he stopped her.

"Wait here, Sue. Let me walk through." He stared her down, watching until she nodded. "You're the victim here, Sue. Let us do what we need to do."

The two officers finally approached her, grim looks on their faces.

"Sue, your place has been trashed and trashed good. I don't know how they managed it in such a short time."

"There would have been more than one, that's a given." She sighed, looking down at her running clothes. "This is not how I planned my day, you know."

They grinned at her, even as they watched the team head for her home. She shook, knowing someone really was after her.

Caleb watched for a moment before he approached her.

"Sue? Come with me. Hannah asked that you come to our place."

She sighed. "Might as well. I need to get some clothes, though."

Caleb reached for her arm, stopping her forward movement. "Peg is looking after that. Eddie called her."

"Eddie? Where is he?"

"He's at the office. He saw you earlier and figured you would need something." Caleb's hand on her arm drew her away. "I'll bring you back. It's going to be a while, I suspect."

She sighed once more. "I know it will." She turned, her eyes searching. "Whoever did it? They're still here. Watching. I want them, Caleb. I want to know why."

"So do we, Sue. So do we."

—

Caleb returned to Sue's house, meeting Eddie, not sure on what was going on. He suspected Sue was hiding something from him but couldn't ask her. Eddie looked around Caleb, searching for Sue.

"Where's Sue?"

"With Hannah. She didn't want to go but I made her." Caleb grinned. "She was that adamant that she was not going."

Eddie laughed. "That she would be. I talked to Graeme. He was here. I don't know how he knew but he said God told him Sue needed him."

"He was?" Caleb spun, looking for him. "We need to talk to him."

"He left. I am not sure where he headed. He was muttering about security, protective custody, and running."

Caleb began to laugh again. "He's been talking to Abe, has he?"

Eddie grinned. "I suspect so. That seems to be the standard line for our couples." He nodded towards the house. "We'll need Sue to go through there. I talked to one of the patrol officers. He was really upset and shaken. I guess there is a threat spray painted on her living room wall. It wasn't enough just to trash her home."

"There was? I don't like this, Eddie. Who did Sue anger?"

Eddie shrugged. "It could be anybody. We're going back over her cases. She's working with us on that, looking for anyone who had threatened her to this point. But, somehow, I don't think we'll find an answer there. It has somehow become connected to Graeme and that house."

"I know. I don't like this, Eddie. How do we keep her safe? She's not going to stop working, we both know that. And that means she's out and about on her own." Caleb began to pace, his agitation and worry showing.

"Graeme told me she wouldn't be on her own in her off hours. He planned to spend as much time with her as he could."

Caleb nodded. "I figured he would. You can feel the attraction between the two of them."

Sue rose from the kitchen table as she heard Caleb greeting his oldest son, before she spun back to stare at Hannah. "Hannah? Did God tell you who?"

Hannah laughed. "Not this time, Sue, or at least not yet. He may and then again, He may not."

Frowning, Sue looked puzzled. "I don't get how He did that with you. Can you explain that?"

Hannah shrugged, even as her eyes met Caleb's. "I can't, Sue. I don't know that anyone would be able to. It's just how He works."

"I don't understand, Hannah. Why?"

Caleb spoke, causing Sue to spin around to stare at him. "It's who He is, Sue. No one can explain why He uses people like He does. It's part of His sovereignty." He paused, his eyes assessing her. "We need you to come back to your place and go through it. Before you do, I should warn you. There is a spray painted threat on your living room wall. It's a given you won't be staying there for now."

She sighed. "That's what I thought you would say. I'll find somewhere."

"Abe called. Somehow, he knew. God was there, Sue. He offered you a cabin to stay in for now."

She shook her head. "He means well, but I can't. I'll find somewhere or else just hole up in a room at home." She walked away, leaving him staring after her.

Chapter 19

Her arms wrapped around herself, Sue stared at her home, devastated at the destruction. It was her sanctuary, a place she came to, to unwind, to feel safe, to have security. Only, it wasn't that any longer. That had been taken away from her and she didn't like that one bit. She knew she'd have to move, that she couldn't stay there any longer. But where did she move to? She could heard Caleb and Eddie and their quiet conversation. No, she couldn't talk to them. They'd just want to stick her away somewhere safe, and she had no idea where that would be.

Hearing a throat softly clearing beside her, she spun, her hand to her throat, before she relaxed and then walked into the arms held open for her. Graeme had approached her, knowing she was terrified and trying hard not to show it. His arms wrapped around her as he began to pray, feeling her relaxing against him as he did so.

Caleb had turned as he heard the footsteps, his eyes watchful as he saw Sue turn to Graeme.

"She needs him, Caleb. Let's pray he's not the culprit." Eddie spoke from beside him.

"No, I don't think he is. I've talked to Abe. He knows him. Said he would never hurt Sue. He saw the attraction between the two at college."

Eddie nodded. "It's there all right. I just don't know if Sue will ever let herself get close to anyone."

—

"What do you mean, Eddie?" Caleb turned to study him in turn.

Eddie shrugged. "She's closed off a portion of herself. She doesn't let us close, not like the others do or have. She's afraid of being hurt, of being tossed aside. Someone needs to find out why."

Sue finally turned in Graeme's arms and sighed. "There's a lot of work to do, Graeme. This is not how I planned my day."

"No, it's not. Abe called. He's on his way in with some of the guys and their ladies."

Sue nodded. "I knew he would. Now, he'll want to stick me away somewhere safe or else have Ian fly me to somewhere no one can find me." She sounded disgruntled, hearing Abe laughing at her.

"That we can do, Sue, but you're not ready for that." He looked around, sharing a look with Murphy, Adriel and Nathaniel. Emma, he knew, was on her way, stopping to leave their son, Isaac, with Peg.

"Where do you want us to start?" Adriel's arm came around her friend as Graeme stepped backwards, heading for Caleb and Eddie, a question on his face

"I don't know, Elle. I really don't know." She looked around, tears in her eyes that she was desperately trying to hide.

"I think we'll get rid of what is broken or damaged first, Sue." Murphy spoke up. "We'll document it for your insurance and then go from there."

—

Three hours later, Sue stood, Graeme's arms around her once more, as she studied her home. It had been cleaned, paint covering the threat on her wall, but she still felt uncomfortable. She knew Joseph had been through at Abe's request, tightening her security system and making her home as safe as he could. Micah had helped. She didn't know where the rest of the team had been but she was sure she had heard their voices over the day.

"I can't thank you all enough." She looked around at her friends and the coworkers who had shown up, uninvited but welcome nevertheless.

"Never a problem, Sue." Murphy spoke for the group. "Now, is there anything else for tonight?"

She shook her head, moving away from Graeme thank each one before they left. She closed and locked the door behind her, resting against it for a moment, before she headed for the kitchen. She needed some of her poison, as Murphy called it, her herbal tea. She stopped, watching as Graeme moved around her kitchen, completely at home. He turned as he heard her footsteps, a quick smile coming to his face.

"Sit, Sue, unless you'd rather shower and change first."

"That sounds like a plan. I have a grill, Graeme, and there should be meat in the fridge." A look of horror came across her face. "We never checked that."

"It was checked, Sue. Nathaniel looked after that. In fact, I think he did a food run for you."

"And he won't take a cent for it, that I already know." She walked to the fridge, pulling open the door. "Nathaniel! He must have bought out the store."

Graeme laughed as he headed for the door, the doorbell catching his attention, back with a bag in his hands. "Here. Mac sent supper for us."

"And he'll have sent our favourites. Let's eat outside."

Graeme sat, watching Sue in the dimming light, knowing he needed to leave but not wanting to.

"I need to go soon, Sue. I'll pick you up tomorrow?"

She turned, her eyes assessing him, before she nodded. "That sounds like a plan. Now, let me walk you through the house."

He stopped on the front porch, hesitating. "Lock up after me, Sue. You need to rest. You're getting brittle right now from today. Talk to God."

She tilted her head to watch him. "Thank you, Graeme. I know you are all praying for me, but this helps. We'll talk tomorrow. I know that's what you want."

—

Chapter 20

Frankie searched the church the next morning, looking for Sue. When he couldn't find her, he searched for Graeme. He knew from Graeme that they had planned to be there. He stood, rubbing at the back of his neck, not seeing Eddie watching him before both Eddie and Caleb approached.

"Frankie?"

He spun, his eyes on Eddie and then Caleb. "They're not here. Graeme was adamant that they would be. I'm off to look for them." He was gone before the other two men could speak.

"I don't like this, Caleb. Not after yesterday."

"Nor do I, Eddie. Let's get our families home and then join the search." He groaned, a remembered commitment coming to mind. "I can't. I have that dinner with Hannah's people."

"Go to it. We'll look. Just keep your phone handy."

Eventually standing in front of Sue's house, the two men stared at one another. They had not found them.

"Sue's car is here." Eddie ducked to look inside it and then walked around it.

"Graeme was picking her up. They had full intentions of being there this morning." Frankie had a

---

bad feeling. "I stopped at Graeme's trailer. There's no sign of his vehicle and no answer."

"Then, where are they?" Eddie pulled out his phone as it chimed. Frankie watched as his face whitened before he stuck his phone back into its holster.

"Eddie?"

"They found Graeme's truck. Out near the quarry. The responding officer found blood on the driver's seat."

Frankie was pulling Eddie with him. "Leave your car. Let's go."

Caleb approached the two later, his eyes raised to the quarry wall and then back to his detectives.

"Frankie? Eddie?"

Eddie shook his head. "No sign of them. We've had the K-9's out but they track just a short way and then lose the scent."

"So, we can safely assume they've been taken to another vehicle and transported somewhere." Caleb began to pace. "But who? And why? Did we ever get to that point, a reason for this? Or ever decide which one they were after?"

Frankie shook his head. "We never did. That's the problem. We don't know which one. It seems to come back to that house Graeme is working on but why?"

Abe's voice startled them. "I can tell you why. It used to be a bootlegger's house. Emma's been able

—

to track it back. He was to have hidden a fortune there, but his family says no. She's working on finding more information for us."

"Do you have a name, Abe?" Caleb's quiet voice barely broke through the stillness that had surrounded them, the barks of the dogs' quieted and the sound of the forest starting to come back.

When Abe spoke the name, their eyes met and Eddie's then slid closed. "Him? Of course, it would be. How do we now prove that? And where do we find our friends?"

Caleb shook his head. "Head for the office. We'll start pulling resources. We'll have trouble keeping it down in number, with one of our own involved."

Abe waited until the other two had left before he spoke. "Emma's finding things on the one who hired Graeme. He's hiding something and she and Jace are working their magic to find out why. The purchase of the house wasn't in his name but a numbered company, which is layered in numbered companies."

"Of course it would be. Tell her to send me what she finds. I'll pass it on." Caleb paused, a prayer rising for his friends. "I don't like that she's disappeared so quickly to finding the threat."

"That bothers me, Caleb. Why trash her house? Why the threat? It doesn't go with what had happened to her. She said she hasn't been getting anything threatening. No voice mails. No texts."

—

Caleb nodded. "That is a concern. I have Grace looking into that. She thought she might have more information by tomorrow." He scanned his watch. "Head on out, Abe. Keep me updated. And tell your guys thanks for searching too."

Abe gave a quick grin. "You know them well. We'll talk again tomorrow."

Caleb watched his friend walk away, before he turned back once more to the activity around him. He knew the trail could go cold and go cold quickly, with little evidence of who had taken them or why. He sighed, his heart once more raising in prayer, asking for knowledge to find them and safety for his friends.

Chapter 21

Three days later, Caleb stood in Eddie's office, waiting for him to find the file he needed before they headed for Frankie. They had not found Sue. In fact, she seemed to have disappeared completely from town. Graeme was the same. They had searched, talked to his father, who insisted on heading their way. They were at a loss. The morale in the building was discouraged but determined to find the two.

Frankie looked up, a finger in the air, as he listened to the person on the other end of his phone call. He carefully set the receiver back on its base and then looked down at his scrawled notes.

"I just had someone call, someone who seems to think they know where Sue and Graeme are."

Caleb studied him, before shooting a look at Eddie. "How reliable?"

Frankie shrugged. "That I am not sure of. I have never spoken with this person. She seems to have called from a pay phone in the downtown area."

"Downtown? As in your old haunts?" Eddie watched Frankie closely, referring to Frankie's time as an undercover officer working the downtown area of Riverville.

"I think so. I'm not sure though. The whole conversation was bizarre. It was like she was on a

---

fishing expedition to try and find out what we knew." Frankie's frown deepened.

"Then it likely was." Caleb pointed to the file in Eddie's hand. "Eddie, explain to Frankie what you just did to me."

"Frankie?" Eddie had to say his name twice before Frankie looked up, shaking his head to clear it. "That woman? She's likely the one our patrol officers have been tracking. They have found one around Graeme's trailer and the same one around Sue's place. She's gone before they can stop her and bring her in."

Frankie stared at him for a moment. "A plant. That's what she is. A plant. But who did this?"

Caleb shared a glance with Eddie. "I would suspect Peter. He's not being upfront with us. In fact, we can't find him at all today. His wife has given us addresses and contact numbers. The numbers don't work. He's not where she said he would be."

"So, is he the one or is she the one being dishonest?" Frankie's voice died away. "That's her. She's the one who called. I recognize her voice now."

"Peter's wife?" At Frankie's nod, Eddie was gone, heading for the desk officer to put out a call for her to be brought in.

Frankie stood an hour later, watching as Peter's wife moved restlessly in the interrogation room. He turned as the door opened and Grace approached him, handing him a file before she silently moved away. He hadn't liked the look she had given him.

Opening the file, he began to read, his eyes raising to study the woman in the room, before he headed to find Caleb.

"She's involved, Caleb." Frankie's words had Caleb's hands freezing on his pen.

"She is? How?"

"She's a great niece of the original owners. No, further back. Her name is different. Peter never likely knew." Frankie turned as he heard a tap at Caleb's door.

Caleb' eyes narrowed as he beckoned the patrol officer in. "What have you?"

"We found the homeowner, Peter? He's being taken to Emergency."

"What happened?" Caleb was on his feet, ready to move.

"A hit and run, by the sounds of it. One of our officers found him outside the old mill. We're not sure when, but we think sometime earlier this morning."

Caleb nodded. "Have an officer stay with him at all times." He watched the officer walk away. "Frankie, head over there. Talk to him as soon as you can." He looked around, reaching for the file in Frankie's hands. "I'll give this to Eddie."

Eddie sat, his eyes on the younger woman across the table from him in the interrogation room, her lawyer beside her. He didn't speak, just watched her, his hands resting on the folder. She moved restlessly, her eyes on him and then flittering away, to come back to his face again. Her lawyer waited, a frown on his face as he watched first his client and then the detective.

"May? Why?"

She sneered. "Why what? Can I leave?"

Eddie stared her down, watching as her eyes dropped even as her fingers tightened against one another. Without a word, he opened the folder, laying the top page in front of her.

"What's this?" She flicked a finger at it, even as her lawyer reached to turn it so he could read it.

"May? What is this?"

"Lies, Everett. All lies."

Eddie didn't say a word, just kept laying the documentation in front of her, including photos. She paled with each one, her voice dying away in its complaints. Her lawyer studied each one, and then her.

"May? This is not good. They have an abundance of documentation and proof against you. What did you do?"

She just shook her head, refusing to speak. Her lawyer, despite his best efforts, could get no answer from her. He finally stood, his eyes on her, before he looked at Eddie.

"I am quitting as her lawyer. She'll need to find another. I have a conflict of interest here, Eddie, as you can see."

Eddie stood as well, tidying the documents back into the folder before he nodded at the door. "I agree,

Everett. She'll be in here for a while. The judge is
setting her bail quite high."

Chapter 22

That Sunday morning, Graeme had arisen, showered, shaved, and then dressed, reaching for a favourite plaid shirt, his hand pausing on the soft flannel. A soft smile lit his face as he remembered his mother's words about the shirt, how she liked him in it, the blues and soft grays the right combination. He reached for the coffee pot, pouring a mugful and then heading for the chair he had stationed at the back of the yard, his Bible in hand. The soft sounds of the early morning filled his ears as did the scent from the roses. He paused for a moment, tucking the Bible under his arm, as he touched a soft yellow and white rose, his thoughts drifting to the day ahead. He would spend it with Sue. He looked up, a prayer in his heart for his lady, someone he wanted to get to know better, already knowing he wanted her in his life forever, God willing,

Parking in Sue's driveway, he had paused before he left his truck, his eyes on her house, a frown on his face, trying to determine just what made him afraid that morning. He finally shook his head, reaching for the colourful bouquet of flowers, in which he had mixed some of the roses from the garden at the MacKay house. He hadn't asked, but he knew Peter would have just smiled and told himself to take them. He had come to know that about Peter. He frowned once more, thinking about the man. His wife, now, that was another story, he thought. I don't trust her and I don't know why.

Graeme tapped at her door, then heard her heels clicking across the floor as she approached, opening it. He stood for a moment, overcome with her beauty, and then simply swept her into his hug, feeling her surprise and then her arms tightening around her. He stood back, his eyes on her face, taking in the smile she had for him, the happiness reflecting on her face. The soft jade sweater looks good on her, he thought.

"You are so beautiful, Sue." He held the flowers up as she hesitated before her smile deepened. "Here. Flowers for a beautiful friend."

Sue looked down at them, her fingers gently touching the petals, finding the roses, before she looked up, a quiet thank you coming from her.

"I'll just be a moment, Graeme. I want to put these in water." She turned from him and then turned back. "I wasn't sure how to dress today. And that is so unlike me. I wasn't sure what you had planned."

"You've chosen well, sweetheart. I plan a dinner away from here and then some time walking along the riverside." He looked at her feet. "You are able to walk in those shoes?" He took in the soft leather shoes she had on with just a short heel.

"That I can." She hurried away and he heard the sound of a cupboard door opening and closing, the sound of water running into a vase, and then the sound of the vase lightly hitting the counter before she came back towards him.

He reached for her hand, stopping her. "We need to pray, Sue. Somehow, I have a bad feeling. We need to reach out for God's protection."

She stared up at him, wondering at his sense of this and then nodded, finding herself wrapped in his arms once more, his voice raising in what she thought of as almost a plea for safety.

They stepped outside, pausing for a moment as she shut and locked her door, then hand in hand, walked down the steps and towards his truck.

Graeme tucked Sue inside, shutting the door behind her, before he heard rushing footsteps behind him and then found himself slammed into the truck door. He felt the knife as it sliced at his side as he moved away from his assailant. He stopped, a hand to the area, before he was shoved around the truck and then into the driver's seat, his assailant taking the seat behind him, the knife now directed at Sue.

Sue's face tightened as she assessed the situation, knowing it might well go bad very quickly. She watched Graeme, seeing the pain on his face and then dropped to his side, seeing the blood seeping through. She spun on her seat, her mouth open to speak, before it snapped closed.

The masked assailant simply shook his head and pointed at Graeme. Sue kept quiet, watching for an opportunity to act, hearing the muttered words of where Graeme was to drive. Her heart dropped as she saw the quarry coming into view. Not there, please, dear Lord. Not there.

Forced from the truck and then towards another vehicle, Sue's hands reached to help Graeme, seeing him stagger as he walked forward. She was forced away from him, and then shoved into the back seat of a car, Graeme into the front seat. She sighed to herself. Classic movements, but I need to get to him. I need to stop the bleeding, and it sure looks as if I can't. Where are you, God? Do You even know what is going on? She felt a peace in her heart, knowing that God did care and that He was there. Why this was happening, she had no idea. She prayed for help to arrive, to find them.

After what seemed hours of driving around, senselessly Sue thought, they pulled into a laneway, driving up to a huge house, and then into the garage, the garage door silently closing behind them. She was dragged from the vehicle, through the house, and up the stairs to a bedroom, shoved inside and the door closed and locked behind her. She struggled back to her feet from where she had fallen to her knees, her hands on the door knob, pulling uselessly to open it. She spun, searching the room, finding no way out. She stared through the windows at the noon day sky, watching closely as the car that had brought them disappeared, with a vehicle behind it. She would later see the second vehicle return and all the men from both vehicles approach the house. They've ditched the vehicle, Sue thought. Now where? Will it be found and then will they be able to find us? She doubted that.

Her thoughts flew to Graeme. Where is he? Was his wound dressed? She paced, not able to settle herself down, not able to set herself free. Lord? Is this what it means to trust? I heard my friends talking about this. Elle and I have talked many times as have Murphy and I. Emma has talked to me to. They all went through such horrible things that I couldn't even imagine at the time. Now, it seems that's what You have allowed. That's it, isn't it, God? You allowed things in our lives.

She turned as she heard the door unlocked and watched as a tray was slid onto the table near the door, the man's hard blue eyes staring at her over his mask, before the door was slammed shut and locked. She heard a door slamming near her and sighed. That would be Graeme's room, now wouldn't it? Lord, protect him. Heal his wound. I don't know who or why.

Chapter 23

Three days later, Sue heard her door unlocked and she turned, finding the man who usually brought her food at her side, his hand tight on her arm, pulling her from her room and down the hallway to another room. She was shoved inside, an office, she thought as she gave the room a quick survey, and then down into a chair in front of a small table. She sat, fear rising within her for a moment before she felt God's hand on her, calming her fears. She heard steps on the floor behind her and frowned. They were unsteady and old sounding, she thought, her eyes on the floor in front of her. She didn't see the man who hesitated behind her before walking around and sitting himself on the other side of the table.

She glanced up, keeping her face neutral and studied the man in a quick glance. Not old, she thought, late 50's maybe. But old in life. His face with lined with the degenerative life he had lived. Hard living, she thought of it. Likely into alcohol, a smoker, hard living. Crime, for sure, given what had happened to them.

Sue sat and watched, assessing the man before her, knowing the man who had pulled her from her room stood just behind her. She could hear the raspiness in his breath. Another smoker, she thought. What have I gotten involved in? Lord, I need you, please.

The man in front of her, and she frowned, trying to remember his name, just sat and then he spoke.

"Well, my dear, where is it?"

"First, I am not your dear. Secondly, I have no idea what it is you are looking for." She stared back at him, her gaze not wavering, watching as he began to move restlessly, his fingers tapping at the table top, his gaze moving from her to the man behind her and then around the room.

"But you see, you do. I have been assured that you have it."

Sue shrugged. "Sorry. I can't help you."

She was finally taken back to her room, shoved inside and the door locked. She spun in a circle before heading for the window, to stand staring out as she had for so many hours, a frown on her face. Where did she know that man from? It had to be from town, but then she wasn't even sure on that.

This walk to the office was repeated every few days. Sue was getting tired of it, but used the time to assess her guard and then the man who always sat in front of her. She had lost track of time but felt it had been a good two weeks or more since she had been taken captive.

Sue searched for Graeme every time she was moved from the room. She listened after her tray of food was left but no longer heard the door to the room next to her opening and closing. Fear for her friend began to grow in her heart. Where was he? Was he alive or dead? She prayed, fear for him driving her words, fear for herself forgotten as she sought to find comfort and peace that Graeme was alive.

Chapter 24

Staring at the patrol officer standing in front of him, Frankie didn't move for a moment, not quite sure he had heard right. The papers in his hand dropped to his desk as he reached for his jacket and ran from the building, heading for his vehicle. He drove rapidly through town heading for the old clothing factory, praying that what he had been told was true, that Graeme had been found.

He slammed his car into park and then shoved the door open, walking rapidly towards Doug Foster, the ETF leader. Doug turned as he heard footsteps, a grim look on his face.

"Doug? What are you doing here?" Frankie was puzzled. It was Doug's day off and he knew that Doug's team was not on call.

"Just searching, Frankie. Just doing some searching. I had word that someone was dumped here." He sighed, his eyes searching the sky before he looked back down. "It's Graeme. He's alive, but not in great shape. Dave and Tom are with him." Dave Allison, lead paramedic, was a good friend of theirs.

"He's here? He's alive? Where?" Frankie turned in a circle, watching.

"This way. He was dumped like so much garbage." Doug led Frankie into the building, skirting the fallen debris as he did so.

Frankie paused, his eyes on Graeme before they raised to Dave.

"Dave?"

Dave spun on his knee for a moment, his eyes on Frankie, before he shook his head.

"He's in poor shape, Frankie. He has a knife wound that is infected along with a high fever. The rain last night soaked him."

"Doug, how long has he been here?" Frankie stepped away, knowing they needed to bring in their crime scene techs and not wanting to contaminate the scene.

"I figure late yesterday. The source I heard from had been in here around noon. It's one of their safe zones."

"So, somewhere in the last eighteen hours or so." Frankie watched as Graeme was transferred to a stretcher and then wheeled past him. He turned to follow, searching for a patrol officer, sending the man with Graeme.

"Now, the work begins. No sign of Sue?"

Doug shook his head. "None. I'm afraid for her, Frankie. I don't like that Graeme was dumped. I am not sure that he was even to be found alive."

"That's my fear, that we won't find her. It's just bizarre how they disappeared. We know they were at Sue's. She had fresh flowers on her kitchen counter. Sue doesn't do flowers. She had also mentioned to Deirdre that Graeme was picking her up in the morning." Frankie walked back towards his car, knowing he had to call Caleb, not sure what to tell him. "What do I tell Caleb?"

Doug leaned against the car, shrugging. "I don't know, Frankie. We're searching. All of us are out there on our own time. Even Abe's guys are doing that."

Frankie leaned his arms on the roof of his car, staring into the distance. "You didn't see anyone who was watching this morning?"

"No, and I didn't feel that either. I think they dumped him, figuring he would die before he was found." Doug shook his head. "Do we even know why?"

Frankie turned his head to Doug, squinting against a sudden shaft of bright sunlight. "That we don't know. There are all sorts of rumours about that building. There always have been."

Doug nodded. "There always have been. I remember when we were kids. We tried our best to find it."

Frankie grinned. "You too? I got in a lot of trouble over that." He sobered. "What I don't get is why did they bring in Graeme? He's not from town. We have many painters who would be able to do the work."

"I know. It doesn't make a lot of sense." Doug stared down at his keys. "I'm heading for the hospital. You'll be here a while, I suspect."

Frankie sighed. "That I will be. If you hear his condition, call me. I have to call Caleb yet."

———

He watched Doug walk away before he scanned the few people waiting and watching. He had contacts here from his undercover days he could go to. He knew they would reach out to him with what information they had. Pulling out his phone, Frankie studied it before he dialed Caleb's number.

"Logan." Caleb's voice was brisk and no-nonsense as he answered.

Frankie squinted at the sky once more, wishing Sue was home and this was all over. "Caleb? It's Frankie."

"Frankie? Where are you? I was just looking for you. I've spoken to Graeme's parents. They're on their way here."

"That's good. I have news."

Caleb froze at the words, not sure if he wanted to hear. "You have news? Which one?"

"Graeme. Doug had someone approach him that Graeme was dumped in the old clothing factory. He came here. The source was right."

"And?" When Frankie didn't respond, Caleb's heart sank. "Frankie? What aren't you telling me?"

"It's just Graeme. He has a knife wound that infected. Dave was the paramedic. He was headed in with him. But I could tell he didn't hold out much hope." Frankie had to pause, to rein in his emotions. "He was out in the rain last night, Caleb."

Caleb drew in a deep breath. "When you're finished there, find me. I'll be heading for the hospital once my meeting is over." Frankie could hear Caleb's footsteps as he walked through the building. "Keep me updated."

Chapter 25

Finally able to head for the hospital, Frankie sat for a moment before he keyed the car ignition to life and drove away from the abandoned factory. He was in no mood for this, he thought. He had spoken with Deirdre, asking her to pray for Graeme and Sue, not letting her know what was going on. He didn't need to. Deirdre knew, he was aware. He parked in the designated spot near the Emergency entrance and sat, jumping at a tap on his window.

Caleb had watched Frankie pull in and then just sit. This is getting old, he thought, and then prayed. His friends needed those prayers. Lord, we have one of them. Where is Sue? Please, dear Lord, keep her safe. And if Hannah were to be told a name by You, please let it be soon.

Frankie slid from his car, his eyes searching. He felt watched and couldn't see anyone.

"Someone's here, Caleb. They know we found Graeme." He turned to walk towards the hospital.

"I know. I can feel that. Talk to me, Frankie. What did you find?" Caleb's steps matched Frankie, his hand out to draw his friend to the side as an ambulance pulled in and backed up to offload a stretcher.

"There's not much. If there was any evidence, it was washed away in the heavy rain overnight. We figure eighteen hours or so, from what Doug's contact said."

Caleb grimaced. "I don't like that, Frankie. And there was no sign of Sue?"

"None. I've put the word out on the street, but so far, no one has come forward. That's unusual. That tells me they're scared."

Caleb nodded, his eyes finding Doug waiting for them. "Very unusual. Someone will contact me, that I do know. There's Doug."

Caleb's steps slowed as he came towards Doug, not liking the look on his face.

"Doug? Talk to me."

Doug looked up. "I spoke with Graeme's parents. They're about an hour out, but they did give the physicians treating him permission to talk to us and to authorize any treatment they deem necessary." Doug stopped speaking, biting at his lip, his face closed, eyes shuttered. "It's not good, Caleb."

"I get that. What did the physicians say?"

Doug looked down, and then back up, a grimace on his face. "It's not good, Caleb. He thinks Graeme was slashed with a knife the first day and had no first aid treatment at all. He's running a high fever. The wound is infected and they need to treat that but they don't think they can take him to surgery to do just that. He's soaked through and through, which brings on chills. That doesn't help his condition." He shared a look with his two friends. "They doubt he'll make it."

———

115

Caleb nodded, knowing that those were his thoughts. "Has someone called Greg, to get the prayer chain working?"

Doug shook his head. "I haven't. I didn't know how much you wanted out there."

Frankie turned as he heard his name. "And there's Greg."

Greg Evans stopped by the men. "I know. You didn't call. God told me to be here." He searched their faces. "Which one?"

"Graeme." Caleb looked up as the physician approached, walking towards him and then following him into one of the rooms.

John Thompson, the physician, was a friend of the men's from church. He hesitated, knowing he didn't have great news for Caleb.

"John? Talk to me."

"Find these guys, Caleb. They're brutal. I am at a loss to understand this." John's hand had reached for Graeme's wrist, checking his pulse before he studied the younger man.

"I know, John, but tell me what is going on with him."

"High fever fed by the infection from his wound. The soaking that has caused pneumonia. Dehydration." John shook his head. "I am not sure if he will even make it. The surgeon's treating his wound. We can't even take a chance of getting him to the operating room. He wouldn't survive that. Then, we'll have to treat the infection and pneumonia. If he survives, it will be by God's grace. Find them, Caleb." John walked away, knowing he had other patients he needed to see, pausing to lean against the wall outside Graeme's room, a hand covering his face for a moment as he prayed. He looked up. Where is Sue, God? Is she alive or dead? Let us know, please, dear Lord. Protect her.

Chapter 26

A week later, Graeme reached for the glass of water on the table by his hospital bed. He was still weak, and he knew he was lucky. No, fortunate, he thought. God had spared him, but for what reason? He hadn't asked about Sue. He didn't want to know that she was around and had refused to come and see him. Dave, Doug, Caleb, and Frankie had all been in to see him, as had Abe and his team. His head went back and his eyes slid closed. He was near to tears, from weakness, frustration and fear. He didn't think God heard him, not any more. He listened to the quiet beeps of the equipment he was attached to, not liking it but knowing it was necessary.

His eyes opening, Graeme stared out the window at the fluffy white clouds passing by, the sunlight coming through that window and the dust motes floating in that light. He could see a wind moving the tree branches and sighed. This was the type of day he wanted to be outside, to explore, and he couldn't. He had no idea how long it would be.

Footsteps stopped beside his bed. He waited, before he turned to look, a frown on his face. He didn't know the man who stood there, a baseball cap pulled down low over his face. Graeme didn't speak, waiting for the man to speak. The man just dropped an envelope on the blanket and the walked away. Graeme watched, his hand reaching for the envelope. He stared

---

at it as he heard more footsteps approaching and then a hand resting on his shoulder.

Murphy stood there, not quite sure what was happened. He studied the envelope in Graeme's hand, not understanding, a frown in place that cleared as he realized what had just happened. He had passed the man in the hallway, not knowing he had just been in Graeme's room.

"Graeme?" Murphy's voice caught at Graeme's attention and he looked up.

"Murphy? I thought you were away."

Murphy gave a quick grin. "Not today. I had to stay around town. Thought you could use some company." He nodded at the envelope. "What's that?"

He shrugged, his fingers rubbing at it. "I have no idea, Murphy. He was here, left this, and then walked away." He sighed. "I guess I need to open it?"

"You likely should." Murphy turned as he heard more steps coming towards them. "Here's Frankie. He can open it for you."

"Frankie can open what?" Frankie stared at Murphy, who nodded towards Graeme. He sighed. "A letter, Graeme?"

"A letter and no, I can't describe the man who left it. He had a cap pulled down too far." He shifted restlessly, feeling the pull from the IV, and then reaching for the nasal prongs feeding him oxygen. "When did they say I could leave?"

"Tomorrow, if you behave yourself." Murphy looked around. "Your Dad said they had to head home, something about appointments they had."

Graeme nodded. "They have already. Mom said they were leaving early this morning." His head went back as his eyes closed. "She's worried about me."

"She's your Mom. Of course she would be. Eddie has told me you're to stay with them." Frankie watched as Graeme nodded. "He's had your camper moved to his place. Your truck is being cleaned."

Murphy and Frankie shared a look as Graeme lay there, not speaking.

"Graeme, I know we've taken your statement. Is there anything else you've remembered?" Frankie was desperate, wanting more information.

The other man shook his head. "Nothing." His eyes searched the two others. "Sue? She's dead, isn't she?"

Frankie's head was shaking before Graeme finished his question. "We don't know that, Graeme. We haven't found her yet."

"I can't help you. I don't remember much. The pain was too bad. All I know is that we were put in separate seats in the car, dragged up stairs and then shoved into separate rooms."

"You don't remember seeing Sue at all? You were gone for about four days when you showed back up in that building."

Graeme shook his head. "No, I don't. Not really. They never took me from that room, not that I

———

know of. I don't even remember being moved and then dumped as you so elegantly put it."

Frankie nodded, knowing from his discussion with Eddie that was what Graeme had said. He looked down at the envelope, finally opening it and pulling out the object inside as well as the letter. He heard Graeme's indrawn breath.

"That's Sue's. It's the necklace she was given on graduation." He reached for it, his fingers stopping short as Frankie shook his head. "I know. I can't touch it. What does the letter say?"

Frankie unfolded the letter, the gloves he had put on making it difficult. His face grew stern as he read it before he looked at Graeme, then shared a glance with Murphy.

"Graeme, again? Do you know anything else you can tell us?" Frankie's eyes didn't waver from him.

Graeme stared at him, then at Murphy, a frown on his face. "If I did, I would tell you. I have no idea why we were chosen for this job. Dad doesn't either. I mean, it's what we do, and we're know for that but there were surely painters here who could do that." He reached for the table by the bed, grimacing with pain as the incision pulled. "Here. Dad left this. This is the information of our company and the work we've done. What is here is public information. Talk to Peter. Find out what he has to say."

"Unfortunately, we can't talk to Peter. He's in a medically induced coma at present from an assault, about the time you two disappeared." Frankie sighed, knowing his workload had just increased. "What we have here is a direct request for your help. From your kidnapper."

"What?" Graeme shoved himself upright, Murphy's hand on his shoulder the only thing holding him in the hospital bed. "Read it to me." When Frankie just looked at him, he reached for it, taking it from him, his eyes rising to Murphy's for a moment.

He looked down, paling even more if possible. He read the letter before looking up at Frankie and then dropping his eyes back to it.

"McDiarmid, you have what we want. We have what you want. Cooperate with us and your lady lives. Don't and you'll never find her body. We will be in touch."

Graeme began to shake, falling back against his pillows, his eyes glued to the paper, watching as Frankie reached for it and took it from him.

"Frankie? What do I have? I found nothing in that house. Absolutely nothing."

"We know, Graeme. We have arrested his wife, you know." Frankie watched closely as Graeme paled even more.

"His wife? Why?"

"That we can't say. It's part of the investigation. However, I can say that she doesn't like you very much."

Graeme shook his head even as his eyes slid closed, and his heart cried out for safety for his friend, Sue, and all his friends. Where does it end, God?

———

Where does it end? I know You're there. I know You care, but I just want Sue home.

Chapter 27

Eddie's wife, Peg, watched as Graeme paced their home two days later, praying for their young friend, knowing it was not easy. A number of their younger friends had gone through this, including their niece, Rebecca and her husband Gideon, and Abe and his wife, Emma. She sighed, knowing it would only get worse before better. Sue had endeared herself to Peg and Peg had taken her under her wing when she had moved to town, praying for her salvation along the way.

"Graeme?" When he turned, Peg beckoned him to the kitchen. "Sit. You need to rest and you can't while you're pacing."

He sighed as he sat and accepted the cup of coffee and plate of toast she slid in front of him. "I know, Peg, I know. I just don't know where she is or why."

"We know that, Graeme. We know that. We have had many young friends go through this." She rose and reached for the pad of paper and pen she kept on the kitchen counter before she sat again. "Talk to me, Graeme. I know Frankie and the others have spoken with you. Tell me why you took this work. How Sue fit in. What the conditions were like in the house. What did you see and not see that you should have."

Graeme stared at her. "You have put it in a way no one else has. Why?"

"Why? Because that's how I think. We need to look beyond what you've said."

He nodded, pushing away the plate that had held his toast and reached for his coffee mug, sipping at the coffee absentmindedly. "So, where then do I start?" He didn't hear the door open and Emma slip in, Peg looking up with a smile.

"Start with your company. I know your Dad started it. When did you go to work for him? Who would have known that you did? This is personal, Graeme, whether you realize that or not. It's not just about this house. Go from there."

Graeme nodded, his head bent over the pad of paper, the pen scratching over it, page after page turned. He finally sat back, exhausted, hearing Peg talking to someone. He looked up to see Emma sitting across from him, her eyes watchful.

"Emma! I didn't know you were here!" He glanced down at the papers in front of him, then shoved them across the table. "Here! You need these. You can work your magic on them. Scare this guy away from Sue and I just like you used to scare our professors."

Emma broke out into laughter. "I wasn't that bad, was I?"

Graeme nodded, a smile hiding in his eyes. "You were. I think we were all in awe of you. I know I was.

I had trouble following your thought processes but you always seem to find your way to the right answer."

She laughed even harder. "I had to. I was raised like that, I guess. I can remember my Dad being like that." A smile hovered on her face as her mind drifted back, before a thought crossed it. "Graeme, did your father ever do work for a computer programmer?"

Graeme shrugged. "I have no idea." He reached for a piece of paper and the pen, scrawling out his father's email address. "Here. You can email him." He studied her. "Why?"

She shrugged. "I seem to remember your father's name and I can't think why." She exchanged a glance with Peg, who frowned, knowing full well that Emma knew why. Emma's attention went back to the pages and she flipped through them quickly, reaching for the pad of paper and pen, making notes before she sat back, her phone out in her hand, her fingers flying across it.

"Emma? Talk to me. Don't leave me in the dark. Please?" Graeme felt like he was begging. He hadn't heard the door open and the sound of men's steps on the kitchen floor.

Emma glanced up past him and then directed her gaze to him. "I have asked Jace to start a search on the names and companies you have listed." She held up her hand at his protest. "There will be no charge, Graeme. We don't charge our friends. You and Sue are both dear and cherished friends. We will search and leave nothing unturned to help you."

———

"She's right." Abe's voice beside him startled Graeme. "It's what she does best. Let her look." At Graeme's puzzled look, he sighed. "I am sure you have heard of Trackers?"

Graeme nodded. "Who hasn't? They seem to be able to find people no one else can." His voice died away at the grin on Abe's face. "No, don't tell me. Emma's Tracker?" When Abe continued to grin and he heard soft laughter around him, he frowned. "You didn't tell me."

"But you said not to." Abe began to laugh at the look on Graeme's face. "She is Tracker. She has Jace and Naomi, a husband and wife team, working for her. They will work their magic or whatever you want to call it. But for now, what do we do for you?"

"For me?" Graeme was puzzled and looked around at the ones who had gathered in the kitchen. "I don't understand."

"First, we pray with you and for you." Caleb nodded at Graeme's look of thanks. "Then we look over what Peg has had you do. She said you questioned why we had never asked you those questions. Likely because we didn't think you were ready for those questions. Peg sensed that you were, that God was leading her to suggest what she did. Emma will work through them. And we can use what she gives us." He looked up at Ben Johnson, a retired officer, who sat beside Graeme. "Graeme, I don't know if you have met Ben yet, but he was one of the detectives until he retired. Ben has sources in town that none of the rest of us do. Ben, first, lead in prayer."

Chapter 28

Late that night, Eddie paced his yard, disturbed at what had been dug up on Graeme's past. Not his past, he thought, but those around him. Which one was the one after him? He knew it had to be someone after Graeme. Sue seems to be collateral to that and that was something Eddie wanted to know the reason for. He turned as he heard footsteps and Frankie appeared beside him.

"Frankie? What brings you here at this time of night?" Eddie pointed to the deck, entered the house and then returned with two mugs of coffee, handing one to Frankie before he sat down in his favourite chair, the sounds of the night ringing in his ears.

"Graeme does. I've heard from the street."

"And that can't be good, to bring you here tonight."

Frankie shook his head, the movement faint in the dim light of the solar lamps. "It's not. I've been told he is to do something, that he needs to do it now. There's a timeline on it. But I don't think he remembers what it is."

"Not likely, given the condition he was in when he was found." Eddie sipped at his coffee, running through what he knew. "How do we get him to remember?"

"I don't think we will. Either he hasn't heard what they said or he's buried it deep. I know Emma's looking into things. She's already shooting me a pile of information that we now have to work through."

"Find the one that the least obvious and the one the most obvious and work in from there." Eddie's eyes slid closed. He was tired, he decided. It was coming up to time for him to decide whether to retire or not. The last few years had taken a toll on him, not the least the danger both Rebecca and Abe had found themselves in.

Frankie stared at him for a moment, his thoughts driving to the list of people Graeme had provided and nodded. "That's how Grace wants to work it. I've let her start with them. I'll pull in others tomorrow. This was supposed to stop, Eddie. We've had enough."

Eddie laughed softly. "I know it was. But it hasn't. Go home, Frankie. Spend some time with your wife. Don't go in until late tomorrow. You need some time to decompress."

"I'll do that." He tilted his head to look back at the door. "How is he really doing?"

Eddie shrugged. "He's a hard read, Frankie. Peg's been able to but she's the only one. He's hurting in many ways, one that he couldn't save Sue. He's afraid, from what Peg said, that Sue is dead. If not, he hates that she's not here and he is."

"They have a connection, Eddie, like many of our friends. Sue never mentioned him."

"Sue is like that. She keeps her friends close, doesn't talk about them by name or in enough detail that we can figure out who they are. She did that with Adriel and Murphy in college, friends with both, neither knowing she was friends with the other."

"That she does." Frankie grew quiet as he finished his cup of coffee and stood. "I'll be in around ten, then, Eddie. Get yourself some sleep. And whatever decision you're trying to make, know that God has the best in mind for you."

Eddie watched as Frankie walked away, his head turning as the back door opened. "Come on out, Graeme. It was Frankie who left."

"It was? What was he here for? Shouldn't he be at home? It's late?"

Eddie laughed. "It is late. He just needed to talk to a friend for a moment." Eddie paused, weighing his words, watching Graeme as he shifted uncomfortably in his chair. "You need to sleep, Graeme. Sue would want that."

Graeme gave a disheartened sigh, the pain nagging at him, knowing he needed to do just that but unable to. "I know, Eddie. Where is she?"

Eddie shrugged, the movement barely visible in the low light. He listened to the night sounds, a favourite time of day for him, usually when he could just sit and meditate on God's words. "I don't know, Graeme. If I knew, I'd go get her for you. But God does. Keep that in mind, no matter how hard it is to trust Him. He is with her, wherever it is she is."

"I know He does. I just want her here and safe."
Graeme rose, waiting for his head to clear, and then
moved back towards the door, Eddie on his feet
watching him closely.

Chapter 29

Eddie rose from his desk the next day, intent on finding Frankie, his mind on the phone call he had just taken from Graeme's father. He searched the building, not finding him, ending up standing in Caleb's doorway, his head turned to look behind before he looked in at Caleb, who watching him intently.

"Eddie?"

"Caleb, we need to find Frankie. He has information I'm told we need to find out from him and I don't think he even knows that."

Caleb was on his feet, moving towards him. "What are you talking about?"

"We need to find Graeme as well. He can confirm what I've just been told."

"Eddie, you're not making sense, and that's not you. What are you talking about? And Frankie was heading for Mac's. Mac wanted to talk to him. Come on. Let's head that way. Frankie's only been gone for ten minutes or so, I think."

Frankie looked up as he saw Eddie and Caleb heading his way, looking past them to find Graeme following them. He sighed as he looked down at his meal. Lord, I just can't catch a break. I need that so desperately. He shifted over on the bench seat for Eddie to sit beside him, watching as Caleb tucked

Graeme in first before he sat himself, Mac heading their way with their beverages.

"Eat, Frankie." Eddie squinted at the clock on the wall. "Lunchtime. Graeme, what would you like? And should you be here?"

Graeme looked up, bringing his thoughts back to the cafe. "I don't know. Physically, my body is saying no. But Dad called. He told me I needed to talk to Eddie. Eddie, why?"

Eddie just smiled and pointed towards Mac. "Here come Mac with our lunch. We eat, then we talk. And, yes, I did talk to your father. A very interesting conversation."

Graeme picked at his food at first, then began to eat, his thoughts drifting from the conversation around him, back to when he had gone to work for his father. His father had not wanted him to, had wanted him to pursue his artistic career. Graeme had taken a look at the books his father had left on the desk, not aware that Graeme had done so.

"I can't, Dad. Not when you need me. You have the Maple building you were working on. You need me to finish that with you. You're just not strong enough."

His father, Graydon, had sighed, knowing his son was right. "I know, Graeme. It's not fair to you. You need to make your own life, your own way. That's what your Mom and I want."

"I am, Dad. I have prayed about this. Friends have prayed for me, without knowing the reason. This is where God has said He wants me, to use me this way." Graeme had stood before his father, strong, tall, young.

Graydon had hesitated and then reached to hug his son. "Thank you, then. But if God says you're to move on, you tell me."

Graeme had nodded, and then turned, his mind intent on the work that was needed to be done. He had worked with his father, until his father's health meant he had to stop, not wanting to. Graeme had set up a room in his father's garage, with desks, computers, and whatever else it was they needed. His father had sourced material, colours, information on the heritage buildings they were asked to work on, not realizing that his son had set this up first to keep him active and involved, finding that he enjoyed digging into the history of each building.

Graeme had stood that day, four months earlier, staring at his father as he leafed through paperwork before Graydon looked up, a frown on his face.

"Why us, Dad? We don't travel to paint, not that far at least."

Graydon had nodded. "I know we don't but this is an exception, I think. We were sought out this time. Word is getting out about our company. I am not sure how, but we seem to be drawing in more work that we can handle. We finally get to pick and choose what we do. We don't have to take every piece of work that comes up." He slid his chair back and rose, heading for the door. "Your Mom will have supper ready for us. Come. We'll eat and talk it over. We'll pray as well."

Graeme followed his father, locking the door behind him, before he stood, his eyes on the sky, knowing somehow that this particular work would be life changing for him. How, he wasn't sure. God, are You there? Are You in this? If so, if we're not to go there, stop us.

His mind came back to the present, and he stared down at his plate, not realizing he had eaten his full meal, not seeing the speculative glances thrown at him.

"Graeme?" Frankie's voice had him raising his head. "What are you thinking?"

"That I don't really know how our name got to Peter. We're not known in this town. We don't have a website or anything like that for people to go to. We work by word of mouth. Our historical society sometimes passes our name on, but not usually. So how did Peter get our name?"

"That's one thing we're working on. Unfortunately, Peter still can't tell us. And his wife is under arrest."

"She is? Okay, so now what?"

Eddie shook his head, not sure how to proceed. "I talked to your father. He's going to email what he has for documentation, although he says you have it saved to your laptop."

"I do, but my laptop seems to have disappeared. No one can access it, though. I made sure of that."

———

136

"That's not good.   You've searched your camper?" Frankie spoke up, his eyes narrowed as he thought through the possibilities.

"I have, but not thoroughly. It just wasn't where I left it. I don't remember taking it to the truck that day."

"It wasn't in your truck." Caleb spoke up. "Your truck is back at Eddie's. Unless you had a secret compartment our techs couldn't find."

"Actually , I do. I'll look in it later." He searched the faces of the men with him. "Eddie, you said you talked to Dad?"

"I did. He's as confused as you are as to why you were asked to take on this work. And it was specific, he said. It had to be you, not anyone else. Why?"

Chapter 30

Watching as Graeme pulled the backseat in his truck forward and felt for a latch on the back wall, Eddie shook his head. No one would have found that, he thought.

"It's here, Eddie. No one found it." Graeme pulled his laptop out as well as a pile of files. "I was searching, I think, that Saturday night. I can't remember completely." He handed them to Eddie before shoving the seat back into place and then locking the truck doors as he closed them. "I'm not sure what I was up to."

Eddie nodded, his eyes moving to watch Frankie. "We'll look these over. Surely, we can help you figure out what you were up to."

Peg watched the men, knowing they had forgotten to eat supper, and sighed, an eye on the clock. She needed to leave for a meeting but was hesitant to, finally reaching for her phone to call and say she just couldn't make it that night. She felt too strongly she was needed there. The Lord always impressed her strongly in situations like this and she had learned to listen. She sat beside Graeme, reaching for the papers as he turned them over, a frown on her face as she read through them.

"Graeme, what were you thinking? Do you remember?"

He looked at her, his brow furrowed. "I'm not sure now, Peg. Something has been off about this job all along. Dad and I couldn't figure it out. Why us? There are surely companies in town that could have done this and at a lower cost."

"That they could have, but you were chosen. Someone has a hate on for you or your father, I would say." Eddie watched as Graeme's eyes slid to his before he looked down at the paper he held.

"Like this?" Graeme handed the paper to Eddie. "I think this was where I had gotten to when I stopped for the night."

Eddie took it, his eyes assessing Graeme, seeing the pain in his face, and knowing that no matter what was said, he would not give up, would not stop as long as they worked. Eddie stared down at the page, his mind already working through the name and its connection to the McKay house. Graeme, what did you do? You're not from here, so you wouldn't know this name. You have just made more work for us. This person has hidden his connection. He pulled out his phone as it chimed. Now what was Emma up to? He sighed again, seeing that she had connected the name and the house and Graeme's family.

"Eddie?" Frankie's quiet question caught his attention.

"Frankie? Emma just confirmed this." He handed over the paper. "She's sending it to you as well." He looked over at Graeme, rising and walking around to draw Graeme to his feet. "Graeme, you need to rest. Sue would want you to. You've just been released from hospital in the last couple of days. You need to get your strength back."

Graeme stared down at the papers. "I know, Eddie. I know she would. I just think there's something there, in all those names, companies, whatever that I'm missing. Something that will find her and find out why she hasn't been released. What do they want from me? I'm not know to this town. Why?" He turned and trudged away, a hand holding his side, not willing to admit to the pain, but knowing he would have to take something.

Eddie watched him walk away, a frown on his face, before he reached for the paper from Frankie. "There's something wrong about that name. I'm not sure what, but it isn't quite right. I know Emma's been finding things on this one, but there should be another name."

Frankie pulled out his phone, reading the text message he had just received. "It gets worse, Eddie. Graeme's father just sent me a text. Someone tried to break into their office in the garage. He's worried about Graeme's mother."

Eddie nodded. "Find out who to talk to in their town. We'll bring them here. Abe's guys will do that. They have all offered. Murphy's hurting."

"He is. I'll talk to Abe in the morning. Graydon had said he wants to move this way, that there really isn't anything to hold them there, other than their business. He said Graeme's been restless the last year or so. Graydon is thinking of closing his company but hasn't said anything to Graeme. He's getting more and

———

more calls for consults from heritage companies. But he's not sure where Graeme is heading with what he wants to do."

"I don't think Graeme knows. But this will be a catalyst to that. He'll not be wanting to go too far from Sue." Eddie tidied up the papers. "Go, Frankie. Get some sleep. We'll take this up in the morning." He groaned. "Tomorrow's Saturday. Peg and I have to be out of town."

Frankie grinned. "That's okay. Deirdre and I will entertain Graeme. In fact, we'll take him out to Abe's. If the guys pack up his parents tomorrow, I know Abe will want them out there."

"That he will." Eddie sighed again, his eyes on Frankie. "We've had too much of this, Frankie. Too many of you young people in danger."

Frankie sobered. "I know, Eddie. It just doesn't seem to end." He looked towards the hall. "And Graeme is hurting. I just wish I could find Sue and bring her back. She's never ever said anything but there has always been a reluctance with her to date. I don't think I've seen her go out with anyone. I wonder if it's been Graeme all along."

"I suspect it has. And the same for Graeme."

———

Chapter 31

Graeme stood on Abe's back deck the next morning, impressed with the land, and the buildings, seeing how Abe had laid out his property.

"This is nice, Abe."

"It is." Abe perched on the deck railing, his hand reaching idly for a climbing rose bloom. "Emma's made changes in our yards. The houses you see are for my team. They were just cottages at one time but as each man married, we expanded and renovated them, making them into homes. Emma calls this Our Haven of Rest, and it is. I'll show you are training facilities later." He nodded towards the lake. "We have the lake as well as the surrounding hills and rocks."

"I can imagine that would be difficult to control anyone coming through that way."

"It has been." Abe shifted. "How are you really doing, Graeme?"

Graeme shrugged. "I have no idea. We were working last night trying to sort through things. Emma's been sending information on, I know." He looked down at the fingers he was rubbing together, a frown on his face. "Thanks for sending your guys for my parents."

Abe shrugged in turn. "Murphy was really worried about them. I understand from Frankie they've had some troubles."

"They have. Dad's not up physically to this. He's wants to retire, but doesn't think I know that."

Abe nodded. "I hear you. He doesn't want to leave you without something to do." Abe turned as he heard a sound, listening for a moment as he heard little Isaac, his son, talking to their cat. "Have you thought about painting?"

Graeme shrugged. "I might. It's what I took in college, all the arts courses I could. It's been a while, though."

"Get through this and then make a decision. Right now, you're not ready to do that." Abe turned more as he heard footsteps approaching. "Frankie? You're here?"

"I am. I needed to talk to both you and Graeme. Can we sit?"

Graeme watched as Frankie sat, not saying a word, before he heard Abe begin to pray, Frankie following when he finished.

Frankie looked at Graeme, then at Abe. "First, Graeme, I just need to let you know that Peter died last night. Someone got to him."

Graeme sat, shock on his face. "He's dead? Who?"

"His wife, we think. We're looking into that."

"Just how does his wife play into this? That's what I want to know. Is she behind this, everything that I've gone through, the one holding Sue?" Graeme felt the anger rising in him and tried to tamp it down, unable to.

———

"It's okay to feel angry, Graeme. We all have at some point." Abe looked over at Frankie. "What can you tell us?"

"At present not a lot about her. We're working through that. She definitely is not who she presented herself as. I doubt Peter ever knew her true character. They had only been married for about a year or so."

"Only that long? I thought longer, for some reason." Graeme stared at Frankie. "That's the impression she gave. Peter never said."

"Peter was a quiet man, never sharing a lot of personal things." Abe reached for his phone, scanning the text message. "Your parents are packed up and on their way. We'll store their things for now, until they find the place they want."

"I can't thank you enough, Abe, for doing this. Now about Sue? What word do you have, Frankie?"

Frankie shook his head. "Whoever it was that took you two is hiding only too well. We have heard nothing about where she is. No hints at all. That fact in itself is very unusual. That tells us that whoever it is has power and money. I just wish I knew who."

Graeme studied him, seeing the strain he was under. "I have a name. I can't tell Dad. It would destroy him." Graeme named the person, leaving the two men staring at him and then at each other. "The good Lord help me, if it's true. It will destroy our family. God knows who it is. I just wish He would confirm this and bring Sue home."

———

"Are you sure?" Frankie's suspicion had been confirmed but he would not tell Graeme that. "Do you know where he has properties?"

Graeme shook his head. "I haven't seen him in years, not since I graduated. He was there that day." Graeme's eyes slid shut as he remembered. "He kept watching me, kept watching Sue, kept watching our friends. I think he was planning something even then. But I had no proof. Once I got home and busy with the company and Dad, I didn't pay any more attention to him. If he's the one, he's had time to plan and prepare." He looked up, sorrow on his face. "Did I do this?"

Abe's hand rested on his shoulder, a prayer audible in Graeme's ear, before Abe spoke.

"No, you didn't. I can remember him, seeing him around the edge of our group. I didn't realize he was related to you."

"No one did. His father was a tyrant. I haven't heard Mom or Dad talk about him for years. I don't even know if he's still alive."

Frankie looked up at that point. "He is, Graeme. He has connections to here. I wonder if he's connected to Peter's wife."

"I am sure he is. That's likely how we got picked for this work. She worked on Peter and had him hire us." Graeme sat back, blowing out a breath, his mind taking in the sounds of nature around him, the faint call of young children, the faint sounds of laughter, the barking of dogs, and sighed to himself. "What did I do?"

"Again, Graeme, you did nothing. You could not have known. We've looked into your contract. Your father asked us to, as well as asking the police department in your hometown. The company that Peter had? It's become buried in many layers. I suspect his wife set it up, not Peter."

Graeme nodded. "That's what you'll find. He said she did the book work. Now what? How do we find Sue and bring her home? And how do I find what they want? There was nothing in that house. All I did was go in and paint. Nothing more than that."

Chapter 32

Hearing the door unlocked, Sue sighed. Here we go again, she thought. What will he demand today? So far, none of his demands have made sense. I have no idea what he wants. All he seems to want to do is talk about Graeme and what he wants from him. I can't help him.

She sat, as she did every few days, in front of the table, a frown on her face today as she waited. She felt today would be a turning point for her, just how, she wasn't sure. A prayer rose from her. She needed to get away, but didn't think she'd be able to. Her hands rubbed along the fabric of the oversized sweat pants she was wearing. The pants and a sweatshirt had been handed to her one day and she was told to change. She had resisted and bore the bruises on her wrists from that encounter. Her feet were in heavy work socks. Her shoes had been removed from her that day and she had been shaken by the violence demonstrated towards her.

She heard the footsteps approaching her and froze, her eyes on the table. She felt his hand on her head and kept herself from cringing away from him. She knew that would only feed his ego if she did so, taking a lesson from the ladies she had helped over the years.

She saw the movement as he walked to sit on the other side of the table from her, the floor shaking slightly under his footsteps. She refused to look up at him, not giving him that satisfaction. Sue felt the agitation from the man and knew today would be it. Somehow, she just knew it was at a turning point. *Lord, I don't know what's happening but You do. You promise to keep me safe. Please, Lord, help me to escape, to get away. I can only hope that Graeme is alive, that he managed to get away somehow.*

Sue looked down as she heard a clink on the table in front of her, staring at the gold bands that appeared in front of her, the man behind her moving back after he had laid them down. She refused to look up or to answer the words spit at her.

"These are ours, my dear. My minister will be here today. We will be married." The wheezing deepened from the man in front of her. "What? Not saying anything? That's okay. You don't need to right now." A cackle came from him.

Sue's hands clenched on her knee as she desperately thought of a way to escape. Her hands found the underneath of the table and laying her hands flat on the wood, she heaved upwards, the table flying towards the man, causing him to shove his chair backwards, the suddenness of her move sending him to the floor. She vaguely heard the tinkle of the rings as they spun in a golden circle away from her. She was on her feet, her hands reaching for the man behind her and her training sending him to the floor, where he lay still.

Sue stood for a moment, hearing the groans and curses from the man who had held her captive before she spun, racing for the door and then down the stairs, pausing for a moment to grab a pair of sneakers sitting by the door. They looked about her size, she thought, as she pulled them on, hurriedly tying the laces, before she was out of the back door and running, heading for the side of the yard and then around to the front. She didn't see anyone waiting for her or after her and she frowned at that. Had there only been the two of them after all? She had no way of knowing, now did she?

She kept moving, driving her feet into the dirt and then into the debris on the trail as she followed it into the forest and then paused, a hand on her chest as she gasped for air, hearing the muting of the sounds around her before the sounds once more surrounded her. Sue listened but could hear nothing behind her. She stared around, her head tiling to study the sky showing through the canopy of the leaves overhead.

Sue knew she had to keep moving but where to, she thought? I can't go back that way. They'll be looking for me. Lord, please lead me. Keep me safe. You provided a way to escape, but I'm not free, not yet.

She kept moving, tired, but determined to make her way home. She finally paused at the edge of a clearing, near a stream, searching for help and seeing none. She dropped to her knees, studying the water, and then carefully drinking. It tasted fine, she thought, was clear, but probably not the best she could drink

Her eyes raised as she heard a noise and she moved backwards into the forest, hiding, her eyes watchful. Sue's eyes then slid closed before she moved forward, a name on her lips.

Ian spun, his hand on Murphy's arm even as he said Sue's name. Murphy turned and then ran towards his friend, stopping to hug her and then standing back.

"Sue? How? Where?"

She shook her head. "Let's move. I don't know if he's following me or not but we need to get out of here." She was tucked between the two men as they moved away from the area. "How did you come to be here?"

"Emma sent us this way. She found this address and wanted us to check it out before she passed it on to Eddie. I don't think she expected you to be here though."

"I shouldn't be." They heard a sound of awe in her voice. "He really did it, didn't He?"

"Who, Sue? Who did what?" Murphy shot her a look over his shoulder. "What are you talking about?"

"God. He got me away from that monster and led you two here today. He really does care about us, doesn't He?"

"He does, Sue." Ian responded, even as he searched the area, not feeling safe. "He cares so much about all of us. We all felt that when we went through what we did."

Sue's voice was hesitant as she spoke. "Graeme? Is he safe? Or even alive?"

Murphy's laugh floated back to her. "He's alive. He almost didn't make it. God's not done with him yet. He's safe with Eddie right now, although I expect he may move to Abe's. We brought his parents back there two days ago."

"You did? They were fine with that? Somehow, I never expected them to leave Graeme's hometown."

"They are fine, in fact, wanted this. His Dad is talking about closing the business, but Graeme's fighting him on that. I don't think Graeme is sure what he wants to do, not just yet."

Seated in Ian's truck, Sue stared down at the clothes she was wearing. She hated them. They were not what she wore.

"Murphy? I need to get some clothes. Can we stop at my place?"

Murphy and Ian shared a look before Murphy turned to stare over his shoulder at Sue. "No, we need to get you somewhere safe. Rebecca has been shopping for you, she tells me. Adriel went with her. We'll take you to Abe's and then go from there. We need to keep you safe and out of sight, at least for now."

She slumped back against the truck seat, blowing out a breath, her eyes watching the scenery passing her window before she frowned. "I was still in town?"

"You were. Somehow it was kept so quiet that not even Frankie's sources knew where you were, other than a rumour you were around somewhere." Ian turned onto the road leading to Rebel's, their destination. "Graeme is with Eddie for now. There's talk of moving him out here but he's been resisting us. His parents are here."

———

Sue nodded, suddenly exhausted. "That's okay, guys. I don't want to see him right now. All I want is a shower and some clothes that fit and then sleep. I haven't slept much in the last few weeks."

"We get that, Sue. Just talk to Matt and let him look you over and then you can sleep." Murphy's hand was on his phone, asking Matt, their team paramedic, to meet them at Abe's.

Sue slipped from the truck seat and then stood, breathing in the fresh air, before she headed for the stairs of Abe's home, her steps hesitant, not sure like they usually were. Murphy steps matched hers, his hand under her arm to support her, his eyes raising to see Abe standing at the top of the stairs, his sister, Rebecca, standing just inside the door, waiting for Sue to approach. Murphy's head shook at the question on Abe's face, knowing they would need to talk, and knowing that Abe would call Frankie and Eddie to come out.

Chapter 33

Staring down at the clothes on the bed, Sue's head finally turned to the closed door, tears blurring her vision for a moment. She had not expected to escape, had not expected Rebecca and Adriel to have shopped for her. She was learning more and more each day how God used others to provide for her. She had felt His presence with her, verses about protection that she had heard and didn't think she had remembered coming to mind. She turned, heading for the ensuite and turned on the water, knowing she would enjoy the shower. She had not been allowed that for weeks, and she felt grubby, she thought.

Thirty minutes later, she stood with her hand on the door, the sweatpants and sweatshirt in a bag to hand over to Frankie or Eddie. Sue knew that they would be out there, Abe would have called them. She walked towards the kitchen, hearing quiet conversation that stopped as she appeared. She sighed with relief. Only Rebecca and her husband, Gideon, were there.

Rebecca watched Sue closely, before she reached to hug her. She felt Sue stiffen and stepped back, a frown on her face, before she pointed to a chair.

"Sit, Sue. Here's your tea. Can we get you anything to eat?" Rebecca's voice was low.

Sue shook her head. "This is all I need for now." Fatigue was weighing down on her, and she stared at the mug before she lifted her head. "No, I think I need to sleep. I can use that room?"

"Please. That's the one Abe wanted you to have." The couple shared a look before watching Sue rise and walk away. "She's hurting, Gideon."

Gideon's arms wrapped around his wife. "She is. She's stayed strong to stay aware of what's been going on around her. She's crashing and needs to." He reached for his phone, sending a text to Abe. "She's not ready to talk today. Tomorrow, possibly."

Abe turned early the next morning as he heard footsteps approaching and saw Sue appear in the doorway, a shuttered look on her face.

"Good morning, Sue." He didn't ask how she was, seeing it in her face and bearing.

"Abe? Is there tea?"

He nodded, reaching to make her the tea she preferred. "Here. Sit."

Sue sat, her hands wrapped around the mug, not speaking, not sure what to say.

"Sue?" When she looked at him, Abe drew in his breath. She's hurting, Lord, and I can't make it better for her. Not even Graeme can. "Graeme will be out later today. He is not aware that you are safe. We have kept that under our hats, per se, to let the team go in to where you were held."

"He got away, didn't he? Lewis Blackmore got away. He'll haunt my steps, wanting to kill me. Did you know he placed wedding bands in front of me yesterday, told me his minister was on the way to

———

154

marry us? That's when I tipped the table at him, took down his bodyguard, and ran." Tears sparkled near the surface. She hadn't heard Eddie and Peg enter, nor Peg's quickly indrawn breath. She jumped as she felt arms around her and then relaxed at hearing Peg's voice.

"Sue, what can we do for you?" Peg's voice was quiet as she slipped into the chair beside Sue.

Sue shrugged, not sure of what she needed. Eddie watched her carefully, knowing he needed her statement and that he had to get today.

She looked at Eddie and then back at Peg. "I think I need to talk to Eddie first, Peg."

Eddie sighed, knowing she was not ready to talk but would force herself to. "Okay, then, Sue. Talk to me. Tell me what happened."

Sue began to talk, her voice faltering at times as she described what she had been through, how she had felt, what she had thought. Eddie's face tightened into grim lines as she described the scene with the wedding rings, knowing that even though she was free, she was not safe and wouldn't be until they caught this man. He had talked to Frankie earlier.

Frankie had stood the day before in the doorway of the office in that house, his hand reaching to take the evidence bags with the rings, a puzzled look on his face before he was handed more bags, this time with a description of what the man had planned, and a wedding license application with Sue's name on it. He had shaken his head, knowing this was not Sue. She wouldn't do this.

———
155

He handed the bags back to the tech and had spun on his heel, moving rapidly down the stairs, his phone out to call Eddie. Eddie had agreed with him that Sue wouldn't have done this. But what the meaning was, neither knew or would know until they had been able to speak with her. Eddie had heard from Rebecca that Sue had cleaned up and then crashed, her body not able to handle being free.

He came back to the present, his eyes on Sue as she finished.

"Sue, the rings?"

She gave a harsh laugh. "He planned on us marrying, can you believe that? He really did. I know he had the application for the license. He held it up to me, expecting I would agree to sign it. He had plans, that man, that included me. I couldn't stay there any more. I didn't care if I lived or died. I just had to get away." Tears blinded her for a moment and she felt Peg's arms around her once again in a hug and heard Abe praying. She needed to get away from them all. They were not safe. That much she knew. She didn't hear the new footsteps that crossed the floor, or the chair carefully pulled back. She felt Peg move away and then other arms come around her. She heard Graeme's voice whispering in her ear. That was all it took for her composure to break and she wept, cradled in Graeme's arms, not hearing the others in the room rise and walk away.

Eddie had turned back to watch the couple, a frown on his face. Now what, Lord? Where do we put these two? I know Sue will want to be back out there, hunting for this man or monster as she called him and rightly so.

Chapter 34

Watching Sue carefully, Graeme stood, reaching for a damp cloth and handing it to her. He removed her mug, making fresh tea for her and then reaching for the coffee carafe to fill a mug for himself. He slid the mugs on the table before he stepped away, looking for Eddie, who had been watching the doorway.

Eddie sat beside Sue, papers in front of him, watching her carefully.

"Eddie? That's my statement?" She reached for it.

"It is, Sue. You know the drill. Let me know if we need to adjust anything."

"I doubt that we will. You're too careful." She read it over before signing it and handing it back. "Now, what?"

"No, what is that we let you have time to heal. Caleb won't let you back yet, you know that. We need to find someone you can talk to. Doug's Darcy has offered, if you want. We need to find this man."

"He was gone, wasn't it?" Her head buried into her folded arms on the table, Graeme's arm around her in comfort. "He'll not let me live, you know that. I got away. He's not going to leave me alone, not until one of us is dead."

"We're working on finding him, Sue. It will take time as you know."

She raised her head, a thoughtful look on her face. "It will, but maybe we can speed up the process."

"What are your thoughts? We're not putting you out there, you know that."

"I know, Eddie. I don't want to." Sue shifted slightly to turn her head to Graeme. "And you can't put Graeme out there, either." She turned back to Eddie. "He'll have hidden in plain sight. I can give you a description, but I'm not sure it will do any good. Frankie's people may be able to help, if they're not too scared of him."

"That they may be. Frankie called me just as I was on my way out here. He's coming this way. He wants to talk to you as well."

Sue sighed. "Can we not? I need a few days to process this. Frankie won't let me."

Frankie slid into a chair across from her, causing her to jump at the movement and then frown at him. He grinned briefly. "Sue, we'll let you have time. Today, I am here as a friend and fellow detective. Not an investigating one. We have evidence we're going over. We're searching for him. We found a wealth of information in that room we need to process. That will take some days. So for now, you're on leave. You are a victim. You need to rest, relax, get some semblance of normalcy back in your life. We'll talk, just not right now." He shared a look with Eddie. "What I would suggest is that you keep a journal. Write down anything and everything you remember."

She nodded. "Thank you, Frankie. I know you want to question me. I can't add anything more than I told Eddie. Anything else is pure speculation or impression, not solid fact."

Eddie spoke up, his eyes watching Graeme as he did so. "Sometimes speculation or impression is what solves a case. We've both seen that happen, Sue."

She sighed. "I know. Right now, my brain is too foggy even for that." She leaned against Graeme, not realizing she had done so, feeling safe in his arms. "I need to talk to Greg. I have questions."

"Greg thought you might. He wants to talk to both of you." Abe finally spoke from where he had been standing leaning against the doorframe. "We'll get him out here. But I think, Sue, you need to sleep again. You can hardly hold your eyes open."

Sue yawned, her head burrowing deeper against Graeme. "I know I do, but I don't feel like moving. It's comfortable right here." Her words died away on the men's and Peg's laughter as she slept.

Graeme gathered her into his arms, and stood, heading for the living room. Peg moved with him, piling pillows for him to lean on as he sat on the couch, Sue still cradled in his arms. He gave a quiet work of thanks as she covered them both, her hand resting briefly on their heads before she walked away. Graeme's eyes were only on Sue, seeing the lines of pain and sorrow, of stress and then of relief as she slept, wanting to talk to her but knowing God had given her this time of sleep. He prayed it would be restorative, even as he heard faint conversation around him and steps approaching and then leaving.

Eddie stood for a moment in the hallway, watching the young couple, before his head turned as Abe stopped beside him.

"Abe? What are your thoughts?"

"My thoughts? That we have a lot of work ahead of us to prove this. He has friends in high places, that much I know. They'll help cover his tracks. I've seen him around. Just never expected this from him."

Frankie shook his head as he stopped as well. "That's not the word from the street. His friends are forsaking him. Other than the ones he's been blackmailing and extorting from. Those are reluctant to talk. I'm getting names that I'm passing on to the team to look at." He looked towards the back door as it opened and Emma came through it, a sheaf of papers in her hands. He sighed. "Abe, will you tell your wife to slow down? I just know she has more information for us."

"I do, Frankie, and it goes well beyond Blackmore. He's only the front man of this from what I can see. Why he wanted Sue? He wanted to be more prominent in society here in town and was shunned. The word I'm getting is that he thought if he had a wife of good standing and who was well liked, he'd be accepted. I don't think he expected Sue to act like she did." She nodded towards Graeme. "That's why he was taken out. He thought they were a couple and he had to get rid of Graeme."

———

"That's what we thought, wasn't it? That Graeme was collateral. But that doesn't explain who brought him here." Eddie was frustrated, to say the least, and wanted this over for the couple.

Chapter 35

Staring at the white boards in the conference room the next day, Eddie just shook his head. He had no idea where this investigation was going. At this point, he always had a sense of that. This time was different. Not one of them was getting a sense of where this went. There were not the usual notes, letters threatening the two, the assaults, the packages. Other than the two being kidnapped and Graeme being dumped to die, with Sue kept captive, it was all they had. Even Frankie's sources on the streets were quiet and that in itself was unusual. This was growing cold, Eddie knew, and he did not want that. He wanted the men and women if that was the case to be found and to pay with their own freedom.

Caleb stopped beside Eddie, his eyes on the boards as well, before he spoke.

"How's Sue?"

"Frustrated. Angry. Wanting this over. All the typical feelings." Eddie pointed to the board. "We're missing a piece of information, one that will solve it. Emma's pulling what she can but she says there is something she's not finding, and that's not like her."

"No, it's not." Caleb studied the boards with a frown. "Eddie, who is Blackmore's father?"

"That would be Lewis senior. Why?"

"Because I don't think that's right. I heard he was adopted as a youngster. Have someone prepared a warrant if that's the case and see if we can find his biological parents."

Eddie paused, his thoughts running wild. "That's what I'm missing. Thanks, Caleb." He spun, stopped in his tracks by Caleb's hand. "Caleb?"

"I think you'll find it goes back to Graeme's hometown." Caleb shared a look with Eddie before the older man nodded.

"That makes bizarre sense. It's always felt like a set up to get him. I'll head out to talk to Graydon."

"No, let Frankie. He can go on the pretext of visiting Abe or one of the men. We need to keep this low key. I know you can go as Abe's uncle but for now, let Frankie. I hear tell Deirdre wants to see Sue."

Eddie gave a laugh. "She's still scary, Caleb. She and Sue make a good team. Does Graeme know that?"

Caleb laughed, then paused. "How is Graeme?"

Eddie shrugged. "He's hurting, Caleb. He's hurting physically. He's also hurting because his lady is hurting. And before you ask, she's his lady. I just don't know if she is aware of that. I watched them last night. She's letting him in closer than she has anyone else, not even one of the ladies."

"I can see that. We'll work with that." Caleb paused once more as he rubbed at his neck. "We're going to have to set this aside, aren't we?"

"We are, and I for one don't want to. I want to see it solved for Sue. I'll look into this information and get back to you." Eddie walked away, leaving Caleb staring after him before he turned and walked from the building.

Ben Johnson looked up as he heard feet on the back steps of his house.

"Caleb? What brings you here?"

Caleb sighed as he sat, his hands folding together on the table. "Ben, we've used you for consultations with the department. I need your help with Sue's case."

Ben nodded. "I thought you'd be around. Stay put for a moment." Ben was on his feet and then back again, sliding a folder across the table to Caleb. "I've been doing some digging, just like I used to."

Caleb stared at the thick stack of papers in the folder before he looked up at Ben. "You've been busy. Talking to your old contacts?"

"They've been contacting me. I know Frankie has word on the street to talk to him, but they're protecting him. Word is out that if anyone talks to Frankie, they're dead and so is he."

Caleb nodded. "That's what Mac has said to me in private. We need to protect them both, don't we?"

"All three." Ben pointed at the folder. "I did some research. I found Blackmore's parents. You were thinking Graeme's town?"

Caleb nodded. "Eddie and I had that discussion about an hour ago. Were we on track?"

"You were. Sue knows them."

"She does? How?"

Ben sighed, his eyes raising to study the clouds drifting by in the sky, listening to the sounds of the birds and insects before he began to speak, summarizing his findings for Caleb, who paled at who he was naming.

"That's in here?" At Ben's nod, he sighed. "Who do I give it to that Frankie or Eddie doesn't see it?"

"Give it to Grace. She's eager to help. In fact, she has been by here, talking to me, picking my brains as to where she should be going and who she should be talking to. She wants to do this right, Caleb, so it doesn't get tossed. She's been talking to me over the months she's been on the detective team, not about cases in detail, but just in general, trying to get a sense of what she should be doing. Not many young ones will do that."

"No, she's eager to learn and not afraid to ask for help. I like that about her. She was the same when she was on patrol." He looked down at the folder. "I gather you're willing to consult on this. I'll take this to her and have her talk to you."

"Please, do that. I'm usually around unless Marg needs me for something."

Their talk turned to their church and the recent messages Greg Evans, their pastor, had been giving. Caleb finally arose, refreshed in his heart, heading back to the office, folder in hand. Ben watched him walk away, a prayer rising in his heart for all his friends.

Caleb found Grace in the conference room and pulled her from it to his office, nodding at the chair in front of his desk. She sat, a frown on her face, not sure why he had asked to speak with her in private. Caleb found the chair beside her, his eyes on the folder before he raised them to her.

"I had a chat with Ben." He watched her face tighten a bit. "Thank you for talking to him, Grace. I know you have not let any information out that you shouldn't have. He's agreed to consult on Sue's case." He held up the folder. "This is what he has found in researching the people involved. I am asking you to delve into this, follow the trail he's on, and talk to him. He's willing to do that. He likes how you want the older ones to advise and train."

Grace blew out a breath of relief. "I thought I was in trouble for that."

"Not at all. Ben has always been a source of information and whatnot for us. We lost that when he retired, but not totally. He does consult on cases. Another one to talk to would be Micah's Kataleen. She has a family tree program that she uses for different police departments to help track families. She's already called me to offer that service. Also, Abe's Emma is another one. Use them. They want this solved and solved yesterday."

Caleb watched as Grace nodded, gathered up the folder and walked away. Lord, guide her and guide Ben as he advises. We need to solve this and soon.

———

Chapter 36

Searching for Sue, Graeme walked through the house and then to the outdoors, not seeing her. He searched the grounds, not seeing Nathaniel watching him before he approached Graeme.

"Graeme?"

Graeme spun, startled. "Nathaniel! Have you seen Sue?"

He nodded. "She's in our work office. Come, I'll show you the way."

The men walked that way, Nathaniel's head twisting as he searched the area, feeling something there.

"Nathaniel? What's up? You keep looking around." Graeme had not missed that.

"I can feel something, Graeme. Someone is watching us. They know you two are here."

"Great. How do we stay safe?" Graeme waved at the rocks and hills surrounding the property. "I know you can't put anyone up there. Anybody with any sense would know that."

Nathaniel grinned as he reached for the door. "No, we can't. And we have had assailants come in from that way. That's why Abe wants you two to stay in the backyard of his house or be with one of us if you have to be out of there."

"And Sue is?"

"She is. I was heading to find you when you appeared. Just keep that in mind." He nodded to the door. "In you go. I think you'll find she's using the boards and computers in here to search."

Graeme stopped just inside the door, Nathaniel at his side, his eyes widening as he saw the activity. "I would say she is, but she's brought your team into it."

"It's what we do, Graeme. It's not the first time we've done this." Nathaniel walked away, leaving Graeme staring after him.

Walking towards Sue, Graeme studied her face, seeing the fatigue still there but the determination to solve this and in solving it, letting both of them go on with their lives. Graeme sighed to himself, knowing he just didn't want Sue to go on with her life without them. He knew he had fallen in love with this lady and wanted her part of his life forever, but he wasn't sure she was ready to hear just that. His hands rested on her shoulders, stilling her movements and sending fear through her for a moment.

Her head tilted back as she looked up at him, for a moment fear in her eyes before it changed to something else. Graeme stared down at her, before he nodded, reading what she had to say but knowing she wasn't ready to admit that to him.

"What are you up to, my love?" He pulled a chair out from beside her and sat.

"Tracking this monster, that's what I'm up to. I can't say for the others. He's a nasty bit of work."

"He's all that and more. What can you share?"

Sue sat back in her chair and studied him. "You're the one I need. Take a look at this. You research historical buildings, don't you?"

"To some extent. Just to get a feel for colour and age and style. Why?"

"Because there's something I missing and I think it has to do with the heritage side of this. Why was this building declared heritage by Peter? The council and the historical society have never done that."

Graeme's hand froze. "They haven't? Peter provided documentation that they had. Dad went with that when he agreed to this." His eyes lifted to Murphy, who had been listening to the conversation. "Murphy? Your thoughts?"

"What you said. Your Dad would have looked into that. That much I remember from knowing him. What does he say about this?"

"He can't understand it. He's looking back through his records and emails from Peter. There's something we're missing about all this. How does that monster as you call him fit into this?"

He heard Joseph's voice and looked around, seeing him approaching.

"Like this. I finally cracked through the layers of the companies. Blackmore was listed in the first company as an owner and then that was buried up. Peter's wife is one of the owners as well. I don't know if he would have been aware of that."

Graeme's hand froze as he reached for the paperwork. "Are they related?"

Micah's voice could be heard even as he and Kataleen approached Sue. "They are. Brother and sister if you can belief that."

Sue reached for the documentation. "I can believe that. We need to talk to Ben Johnson." She looked around the men as the door opened and Ben and Grace appeared. "Ben! Just who we were wanting to talk to!"

Ben laughed at her. "Well, here we are. And why, might I ask?"

"Kat's found a connection between Blackmore and Peter's wife. They're siblings."

Grace paused as she was setting down the folder she had carried. "Siblings? I didn't know that."

"It's buried. Blackmore was adopted as a young boy. Peter's wife wasn't." Kat spoke up. "Don't ask how I found it. I can't explain it but I did it legally. You'll have evidence here that you can use to get the warrants you need, Grace." She handed over the papers she was holding. "Take this. I have copies."

Ben sighed as he looked around the office. "I don't know how your team does this, Abe, but they're good."

"I know they are. They'll keep digging." Abe pulled Ben to one side. "Nathaniel said there's evidence someone is watching us again."

"Of course, they would be." Ben turned to watch Sue and Graeme. "And you know those two will make a break for it soon."

"I know they will, and we can't stop them. We don't have enough evidence for Caleb to put them into protective custody, and they won't let us do much more than we are. Sue's too independent that way."

"She is, Abe, but she will listen to you. She'll grant you that. It's just whether she'll do what you suggest."

"And I can almost guarantee you she won't. Graeme will go with her if she runs."

"And she'll go with him if he runs. He's to the point he will. He'll be out there searching for Blackmore."

"And more than likely end up hurt worse or dead."

Chapter 37

A week passed and Graeme felt too confined to stay with Abe any longer. He moved his belongings back to the camper in Eddie's driveway, Eddie standing at the door of his house watching him. Sue stood beside him, not sure where she should be, but ready to go home as well. She was back to work, although confined to the office, and she did not like that. She wanted in on the hunt.

Caleb watched Sue as she strode towards him through the office the next day and sighed. Sue's on a hunt and I don't think I'll like what she has to say. Lord, stop this lady and help her to listen.

"Caleb? Got a moment?"

"I do." He turned back into his office, pointing at a chair as he sank down in his own. "What's going on?"

"I'm not sure, Caleb. You have me going back over some of the older cold cases. There is one that seems too familiar." She handed him the folder, not letting it go for a moment. "I don't understand the link, though."

Caleb read the name on the folder and his heart sank. "This is one I think we never could get a handle on properly. Ben would be the one to talk to. I think you'll find somehow it's connected to you and Graeme."

"That was what I thought." She looked up as she heard footsteps stopping at the door. "And here is Ben."

"Ben?" Caleb looked at him, not sure why he was there.

"Caleb. Sue. I've had word about you, Sue. You and Graeme." He sank into the chair beside her, taking the folder Caleb handed him. He read the name and sighed once more to himself. "And this is the connection. How did you find this?"

"Caleb was having me review old cold cases. This one seemed too close to what we're going through."

Ben nodded. "It is. We tried hard to solve it, but never could. We never had that one piece of information or evidence that we needed to do just that." He stared down at the folder. "Peter's wife was involved in this, somehow. We could never prove it though"

Sue's eyes stayed on Ben, knowing he was processing facts and would speak when he had done that.

"Caleb?"

Caleb was studying Sue but looked towards Ben as he spoke. "Peter's wife? She must have been young at the time."

"She was. A teenager, if I remember. There was something about her we couldn't put our finger on." He looked down and then up again. "I hear you've arrested her, and that she has a string of aliases."

"She does. I'm not even sure we've found them all." Caleb leaned back in his chair, his pen tapping gently at the paper on his desk. "Grace was working on that."

Sue nodded. "She was. She's put what she's found in this folder. I don't like it, Caleb. To have her connected to this case, and then us?"

"No, I don't ether. Ben?"

Ben studied Sue for a moment. "Sue, you know Graeme from college. What are your thoughts as to why someone's after him?"

Sue studied Ben's face, trying to get a sense of why he was asking that, before her thoughts turned to Graeme. "I really don't know. I think it may have something to do with the heritage work he has been doing. His father does the research mostly, although Graeme is starting to do that as well. Graydon was wanting to move it to more a consulting business. That way he could keep working but let Graeme take up his artist bent."

"Artistic bent?" Ben spoke up. "What do you mean, Sue?"

"Graeme wanted to paint, to do portraits and animals. That's what he studied." Her eyes slid shut. "I think I just got the link."

Ben and Caleb shared a glance.

"What link, Sue?"

She shook her head, trying to clear her memory. "Graeme had done some portraits while at college. One of them, if I remember, was from this town. I need to talk to him about that, but I think somehow it was connected to the MacKay house. That place sounded so familiar."

"You may be on to something. Talk to him. Then talk to Ben again. Graeme needs to speak to him as well." Caleb watched as they walked away, not sure if they were on the right track, but even if they weren't, he knew both would keep digging. Protect them, Lord. I just know they'll need that.

Chapter 38

Graeme turned the next morning, hearing footsteps approaching him. He frowned, not recognizing the man who stopped in front of him. Setting the folders down on his chair, he waited, not sure what was happening, but not willing to move any closer.

"You're McDiarmid?" The man's voice was hoarse and low.

"Why?"

"You're McDiarmid?" The man repeated his question. "We know you are. You have something we want."

Graeme shrugged. "You've already tried that. I have nothing you want. I'm just a painter. I don't dig into anything." Graeme felt himself shoved forward and hit the rough pavement with his hands and knees, the jar triggering pain inside his abdomen.

"You have something. You know you do. We want it, or your pretty lady disappears. You have a week to produce it." The man watched as Graeme struggled to his feet.

"I don't have anything. How would I know what you want?" Graeme couldn't duck the blow that was lodged at him, his body collapsing to the ground. He didn't feel himself dragged around the camper and then dumped, a tarp pulled over his body, before the men left

Eddie pulled in late that afternoon and parked, not seeing Graeme. He shrugged, heading for the house, knowing Peg had planned to be away that day. He turned as he heard a vehicle behind him and saw Ben and Sue heading towards him.

"Ben? What brings you by?"

"We're looking for Graeme. Is he around?" Ben searched the area. "Is that his truck?"

"It is." Sue's face grew grim. "It's here. Where is he?"

"I just got home, Sue. I haven't seen him." He walked to the camper, tapping at the door, then opening it and calling for Graeme. "That's strange."

Sue's hands reached for the folders, scanning through them. "He's been busy, but where is he?"

They began to search, Sue heading around the camper, frowning at the tarp spread out. This is strange, she thought, reaching to pull at it, calling for Eddie and Ben as she found Graeme. On her knees beside him, she reached for his wrist, relief spreading through her at the pulse under her fingers.

She stood back with Ben, Eddie speaking with the responding officers, as she watched the paramedics work on Graeme. She finally approached Dave.

"Dave? How is he?"

Dave Allison looked up, first at her, and then Ben standing behind her. "He's unconscious, Sue. I don't know how he is. You'll have to ask the doctors. His parents are in town?"

"They are." She sighed. "They're at Abe's. You know what that means."

Dave gave a quick grin as he stood, raising the stretcher to its full height, ready to move out. "He'll put you both out there and throw away the key, you know."

"That's not happening. I'm riding with him." She turned and was away before Ben could speak.

"Watch her, Dave. Someone's after both of them. We're working on that."

"I can see that." Dave hesitated for a moment. "I heard about Peter. I knew him from Rylee's bake shop. There's something odd about that house. Always has been."

Ben nodded. "I know. I just wish I could figure out why. Grace is working on something for Caleb." He nodded to the stretch. "Away with him, you two."

Graydon watched as Sue paced the waiting room, moving among the people gathered there. He shared a look with Graeme's mother, Eliza, before he rose and walked towards Sue, a hand on her arm stopping her.

"Come, sit with us, Sue. You'll wear yourself out pacing like this."

She studied him, before she turned to stare at the door to the examining rooms, hearing the buzz of conversation around her, the overhead sound system calling for certain physicians and finally nodded.

———

"Okay. I will, just for now." She turned to study Graydon, talking in the pallor of his face, even as he limped back to his chair, his cane thumping quietly as he walked.

"We're okay, Sue, both his Mom and I. We're worried of course. Who wouldn't be?" He sat, a groan not quite covered. "But, the question is, how are you?"

She shrugged. "I'm alive, I guess that a bonus." She studied the older couple, seeing in Graydon a lot of the mannerisms she knew from Graeme. "Has anybody talked to you two?"

"About what, dear?" Eliza shared a look with Graydon.

"About what is going on? How far back does this go?"

Graydon nodded. "I see what you're saying. We need to talk, Sue, and we need that friend of yours, Frankie, is it? He needs to be in on the conversation." He looked up as he heard footsteps, rising to his feet as the physician approached.

Chapter 39

Awakening in the night, Graeme's eyes searched the room, a frown on his face. Where am I, he thought? He reached for the blankets, shoving them off him, before he sat on the side of the bed. He looked around, almost too tired to do so, before he realized he was in the hospital once again. What had awakened him, he wondered?

He felt hands on him, helping him to dress, and then to a wheelchair. He felt himself moved from the room, quiet footsteps beside and behind him, not sure what was going on, but knowing he was too tired and in too much in pain to care. He didn't realize he was being led from the building or that Matt and Luke were on either side of him, helping him to the elevator and then to Ian's vehicle that waited at the back of the hospital.

"Matt?" Ian's voice was quiet as he watched Matt settle Graeme in the back of the SUV.

"He's hurting, Ian. Let's roll."

Ian drove away quickly, all three men with eyes watching for anyone or anything. "Abe has the place ready for us." He drove seemingly in a random manner before he headed for their complex.

"Where are his parents?" Matt watched Graeme closely, seeing the pain and stress on his friend's face.

"Abe has them out there, locked in his house. Rebecca and Gideon are away right now, so he can't use Gideon."

"And we've got that team in for training next week." Luke twisted to watch Graeme as well. "Where's Sue in all this?"

"Caleb's not saying at the moment, but Abe plans to bring her out. She's been talking to Graydon and he wants to talk to her." Matt's brow furrowed. "It seems as if he might have known her father?"

"He did?" Ian slowed as he turned into their home area and then parked near Abe's home. "They connected in more than just college?"

Matt nodded, reaching to help Graeme from the vehicle and then up the back steps to the door, finding Abe waiting for him.

"No problems?" Abe's question was quiet in the night air, the sounds of nature not disturbed.

Ian shook his head. "I didn't see anyone." He nodded at the vehicle pulling to a stop beside the one he had driven. "There's Frankie and Sue. He was behind us and would have taken defensive action if there had been."

Sue walked towards Graeme and reaching out to Graeme, touched his face, not seeing the looks directed at her and then at Frankie, who shrugged.

"Can we get inside, people?" Frankie's question had them moving inside, Matt helping Graeme to a first-floor bedroom.

———

Sue hesitated before she headed up the stairs, knowing Abe had set her up in a bedroom up there. She passed Emma heading her way, a hug from her friend helping, a few soft words before she shut the door behind her. I'm a prisoner now, am I, Lord? How do I work? How do I find the people? I know, You're telling me it's not my job. But my friend has been hurt. Heal him please.

Frankie dropped his briefcase on the table in the living room and then turned to Abe. The three other men had left, Matt promising to be back in the morning.

"Abe?"

Abe turned. "I know, Frankie. I know. You're here when you think you should be somewhere else. But I think Graydon has asked for you."

Frankie nodded. "That's what Sue said. I have no idea why." He sank to the couch, then stretched out, pulling the afghan from the back over him. "Wake me in the morning, will you? I have still have to explain to Deirdre why I'm here and she's not."

Emma made a sound and Abe turned to her, nodding at the look on her face. "We'll get her out here for you, Frankie. In the morning."

Chapter 40

Dropping the papers on the table, Graydon sat back, his eyes on first his son, knowing Graeme shouldn't be there. He had been brought out overnight, and Graydon was not sure he should have been. His attention then turned to Sue, finding her deep in her work, a hand propping up her head, as pen in hand, she read through what Kat had handed her on the background history of Peter.

"Sue?" Graydon's voice caused Sue to look up at him, a finger marking her place in the paperwork. "What was your Dad's name?"

"Dad? He's Paul Walters. Mom's name is Eunice. Why?"

Graydon nodded. "Then I did meet your Dad. Many years ago. He was a builder?"

She nodded. "He was or a renovator I think would be closer to what he did. He used to travel to work. Why?"

"It was him. He was in our town for a while, working on a building. I had been called to put in a bid on it. I didn't get that particular bid, but I did have time to spend with your father. We lost touch."

"You knew Dad?" She sat back, her eyes on Graydon before they moved to Graeme. "I never knew that. Did you, Graeme?"

Graeme shook his head, slowly, waiting for the pain to decrease before he spoke. "No. I didn't. I don't see how that makes a difference here."

Frankie spoke up. "It makes a difference before it now involves both your families. We've been working back through them and had come to that conclusion, that somewhere you two had crossed paths. It was with your fathers." Frankie looked over at Graydon. "Why didn't you get that house to paint?"

Graydon shrugged. "It's how it goes when you put in bids. Sometimes you have the right bid, have a low bid or too high a bid. The owners choose which one they want." He stopped, puzzled, his eyes on Sue again. "But that particular one? There was only one other bid, and it was too low for the amount of work required. But they chose it?"

"You're thinking that something was off, that you were asked to bid just to say there had been other bids?" Frankie watched him closely.

"I do. And I think that paperwork Sue is looking through may have an answer. I know Kat has been busy. I've talked to her." He reached for the papers he had placed beside him, handing them to Frankie. "Look through these. I always keep everything, always. This is the correspondence of that house. And the correspondence on the MacKay house."

Frankie leafed through them, and then back through them, before sitting back, lost in thought.

"Frankie?" Graeme's voice caught his attention.

"Your father has solved one thing for us, but opened up something else. Peter's father-in-law was the one who approached you, Graydon. Is that what you're saying?"

"It is. I never liked him or felt comfortable around him. I know Paul didn't either but at the time felt he had no choice but to take the work. He was just really starting out and needed to provide for his family. Sue, this would have been when you were small."

She nodded, her attention back on what she was reading. "It says here that he is related to the mayor, Frankie."

"He is? That doesn't surprise me. He's been able to skirt bylaws for a while and no one could figure out why. That would do it."

Frankie finally rose, tucking his paperwork in his briefcase, his eyes on the young couple as they walked towards the back door, Sue's hand tucked into Graeme's elbow to help stabilize his walk.

"How serious are they, Graydon?"

Graydon shrugged, his eyes on his son before he looked at Abe, who nodded. "Serious, I think, Frankie. Graeme hasn't been like this since he came home from college. He would bring Sue home every once in a while. We could see the interest there, but we have no idea why they walked away from one another."

"Neither were ready at that point." Abe sighed. "And now they are, just like everyone else."

Graydon agreed, rising to stand at the back door, watching his son and the lady he was interested in. "How safe are they, Abe?"

Abe shrugged. "As safe as we can make them. We have had breaches over the years. We can't patrol all the area around us, but my guys are up there as much as they can to search. We have the safe room we'll get them to if we need you. You and your wife as well."

"Thank you for that, but somehow, I don't think that will work." Frankie waved as he left.

"I think your friend is right, Abe. They are planning on going on the offensive, aren't they?"

Abe grinned. "All the couples do at some point. Why would they be any different?" He turned as he heard Emma heading his way. "Emma?"

"I'm off, Abe. Jace will be by later. He says he has some information for Sue, but he's heading in to find Eddie first. He didn't tell me what it is."

Abe nodded, watching as she walked away, knowing she wasn't saying something and wouldn't until they were alone.

"Graydon, what can we do for you and your wife? How can we make it easier for you?"

Graydon turned. "Your son is helping fill my wife's day. She adores him." He nodded towards the door. "I can find something to do. I have my Bible and am deep into a study of the Minor Prophets. Graeme? He needs something to fill his day. Sue's not going to stay out here. She has work she needs to be doing."

———

"That she does. We'll be transporting her back and forth starting tomorrow. My team will make sure that Graeme is taken care of. That's a given. Their ladies will look after Sue. But that doesn't solve the mystery for us."

"No, it doesn't. I can't think what it is that he would have." Graydon paced, his mind wandering back through the years, before he paused, spinning to find Abe watching him.

"You've remembered something."

Graydon's eyes slid closed, not hearing Graeme and Sue enter the kitchen and stop, Sue's arm around Graeme, his around hers, causing Abe's one eyebrow to raise as he hid a quick smile. *Emma, you were so right. They have become a couple over this, just like everyone else.*

"Dad?" Graydon's eyes popped open and he stared at Graeme. "What did you remember?"

"Not what you would like to hear. I have to go back home to get something."

"Let my team go. Tell us what you want and we'll head there."

Graydon studied Abe before he turned a frown at his son and Sue, before he nodded. "I can do that. What they want to find is a metal box. Here, let me tell you where it is and give you my keys and security code." He grinned suddenly, looking very much like his son. "Didn't think we had that, now did you?"

Abe laughed, as he took the proffered keys and paper. "I figured you would. You're too careful."

———

189

Chapter 41

Sue was restless and needed her run. She didn't like this having to stay hidden away, and she was vocal in her words. Abe just looked at her and shook his head, walking away. Graeme stared at her, a hurt look on his face, before he too moved away from her. She sighed. Her parents had been in touch, and she had refused to let them come near her. Her father had questioned her about Graeme. Hearing he knew his father, Paul had been quiet, and then just warned her to be careful.

She headed for the lake, not telling anyone where she was off to, knowing they would stop her. Her phone was tucked into her arm band, her earbuds in place as she listened to her favourite music. Her stride lengthened as she settled into her run, relishing the breeze on her face.

Not hearing the footsteps running towards her, she was taken off guard as she was tackled to the sand along the lake shore, startling the ducks floating nearby into flight. Unable to fight back, she felt the gag across her mouth and then the ropes as they were bound around her wrist. A blindfold across her eyes shut out the light even as she struggled to escape. She felt herself picked up and carried away, dropped into a boat, and then the boat shoved from shore. Sue felt the boat tip as someone stepped into it and hear the soft sounds of the oars as they dipped in and out of the water.

Sue was dragged from the boat, her feet in shallow water, before she was shoved forward, a hand on her arm to lead her. She spun as the door to the room closed behind her, a warning not to remove her blindfold or gag echoing around her. She felt her way around the room, finding a chair that she sank in to.

Lord? Now what? I was foolish. I didn't tell anyone where I was or what I was planning. Will they find me in time? Please, dear Lord, protect Graeme. I don't want him to grieve for me.

Hours seemed to pass before she heard the door and then the sound of a paper bag being set down. Her hands were freed and the gag removed, but she was told not to remove the blindfold.

She reached for the food, taking the water bottle out and feeling it over, before she drank. She sat back in the chair, her mind working, trying to place the voices. She knew them, she thought, just couldn't put a name to them, and that she needed to do. She saw the dimming of the light around her blindfold and rose, feeling for a bed, laying down and covering herself up, her eyes closing as she slept.

Graeme was on a search. He couldn't find Sue and needed to. His heart raced as he thought through the possibilities. Nathaniel watched him and then approached.

"Graeme? What's going on? You're on a mission, I can tell."

Graeme spun, catching his balance. "I can't find Sue. She didn't go to the office, that I know. Frankie called looking for her."

Nathaniel's face grew grim. "She's not in the house or the backyard?"

"No, she's not." Graeme's face turned towards the lake and he paled. "She didn't, did she?"

"Didn't what?"

"Go for a run. She likes to run and hasn't been able to." Graeme stared at the lake and then headed there as quickly as he could, Nathaniel at his side.

They searched, Nathaniel's hand coming out to stop Graeme. "She was here, Graeme. And taken away."

"How?" Graeme stared at the ground and then the lake. "Across the lake?"

Nathaniel shrugged, his phone out, even as his hand moved Graeme away. "We need to move from here, Graeme. We need to let the police work their way through this."

Caleb stood beside Frankie, watching the activity, before he turned to watch Graeme, who leaned against the large rocks near the lake.

"She didn't tell anyone what she was up to?"

Frankie shook his head. "Not from what I'm told. It looks as if she came her to run and was taken down. We suspect she was taken across the lake, but just where we'll have to search. There are a lot of hidden cabins in there that we will have trouble accessing."

"And it's on Abe's land, isn't it?"

Frankie nodded in agreement. "That's one thing working for us. His guys know this land so they can help direct us. That is, if she's there."

Caleb turned as Eddie approached. "Eddie? I'm not liking that look."

"Didn't think you would. Sue's father was in an accident this morning. He's in a hospital in Oak City."

"That's not what I wanted to hear."

"None of us did, Caleb. Her mother's looking for Sue. How do we tell her that Sue's missing, once more?"

Caleb shook his head. "This is just too strange, you know. Did we ever connect Sue to that house?"

"Not really. I know their fathers had met years ago, but I don't see the connection." Frankie turned, his eyes once more on Graeme. "Although his father seemed to think there was a connection between a renovation he did years ago and this house. Luke and Murphy headed towards their home this morning, to bring back information he had stored away."

"I pray it helps to solve this. We need this over with and soon. Graeme's not going to survive if we don't. He's been talking to me, Caleb. He wants to date Sue but is afraid to right now, thinking he's too dangerous."

"And if it's Sue that's the dangerous one? What then?" Caleb was frustrated, to say the least, turning as he heard his name called.

"Walter? What do you have?"

The crime scene tech shook his head. "I don't think she had a chance, not by what I'm seeing. She was down and then gone in just a few steps. They had a boat waiting for her, likely. That means she's across the lake. Whether she's still there or not, that's the million dollar question." He held up an evidence bag. "We're assuming this is her phone. We also have a note that was dropped. Addressed to you, Caleb."

"To me?" Caleb reached for the bag. "Why me?"

Walter shrugged. "It explains it, I think."

Caleb studied him, then searched the faces of the men with him, Abe having joined them. His eyes dropped to the letter and he frowned. This did not make sense, now did it?'

"Caleb?" Eddie's voice broke into his thoughts, and he handed the older man the letter.

"A trade. Sue for what they have been looking for." Caleb paced and then turned to Eddie. "We need to search that house. Get us a warrant." He pointed at the letter. "That will help us get that."

Eddie nodded and walked away, Frankie beside him. Abe watched and then turned to study Graeme.

"This has never made sense, Caleb. It feels as if we're being sent off on a wild goose chase, headed away from what we need to be looking at."

"That is exactly how it feels." Caleb stood, lost in thought before he looked up. "You're right, Abe. It is to throw us off. Now, what was Sue working on at the time she was taken the first time?" He paled and then turned, running for his vehicle, heading back to the department, leaving Abe staring after him.

"Abe?" Graeme's puzzled voice had Abe turning his head.

"I think Caleb just figure out what's going on. As soon as he knows for sure, he'll be out to talk to you. In the meantime, we need to get you back to the house. They'll be working here for a while, and then my team will be spreading out to look."

Chapter 42

Staring at Caleb and then Eddie, Graeme just shook his head. He didn't understand why they had changed what they were looking at, and they didn't seem to be willing to explain, just asking more questions of him.

"I don't know that name, Caleb. I've never heard it before. Is there a reason I should?"

Caleb nodded. "It's all related to the MacKay house, but this is someone from town. Someone in the civil service here."

Eddie took pity on Graeme. "We're not asking this for the fun of it, Graeme, but at some point, you have crossed paths with this person."

Graeme kept shaking his head. "No, I have never heard of him. Is there another name you want to run by me?"

"There may be kids involved. We need to search your class at college. That may be where you've connected." Eddie pointed to the yearbooks he had asked the men to bring back. "All we ask is that you go through them. See if anyone stands out. If you see the name. This is what may help us find Sue and bring her back to you." Compassion showed on Eddie's face as he watched Graeme struggling to keep his emotions under control

Graeme finally sighed, sinking into a chair at the kitchen table, setting his coffee mug to one side, and reaching for the top book. "I can do that. I'm praying she comes home, but right now, it doesn't feel as if God hears me."

"He hears you, Graeme. It's just that sometimes He doesn't answer as soon as we demand or like or in the way we think He should." Eddie's hand rested briefly on Graeme's shoulder. "Go through these. Call us if you find anything."

"And do you think I will?" He looked up, stress showing on his face and in his voice.

"I think you will, Graeme. I really think you will." Caleb's hand too rested on Graeme's shoulder before he and Eddie walked away.

Graydon had stood to one side, listening, watching his son, his heart breaking for him. "What have they asked, son?"

"They want me to go through these." Graeme's hand flipped towards the books. "They think it's something other than the MacKay house and that was only a diversion."

Graydon nodded. "I think they're right. That has never ever made sense. What did the men ask from you?"

Graeme sat back, his eyes on his father. "They just asked me to turn over what they wanted. They never asked for anything in particular. That's been the bizarre part of this all."

"And now they have Sue once more. Did Caleb ever figure out what she was working on, that might have driven this? And caught you in the middle just because you came to her town and knew her from college."

"It goes back to that, doesn't it, Dad? It goes back to our college. But not the college. The church itself. Who was there then that saw or heard something or did something and thinks Sue knows about it?" Graeme sat back, a frown on his face. "Who is it, Dad?"

Graydon reached for a pad of paper and a pen, looking at his son. "Start telling me names and what you remember about each one. We need to set this down in a logical manner. Tell me what Sue was up to and who she knew that you know about that wasn't directly in contact with you. Somehow, we'll work this through." His eyes raised as he heard the back door close and Kat appeared, laptop in hand. "And here's Kat, come to work her magic." He looked around as he heard the front door. "And who do we have here?"

"Hi. I'm Darcy Foster, Doug's wife. I think you've met him sometime lately. He's one of the ETF commanders on the force. But I'm here as a friend. I used to work as a forensics psychologist. I'm here to try and set up a profile for you, to see what we can determine."

Graeme stared between the two women, a frown on his face. "Why does a psychologist sound familiar?" He rose and paced away from him.

———

The three in the kitchen could hear his footsteps as he paced before they exchanged glances.

"What was Graeme in the middle of?" Darcy's voice was quiet as she reached for the top yearbook.

"He was asked to go through the yearbooks and see if he recognized a name." When Graydon said it, Darcy looked up at him before she nodded.

"Yes, I can see that." She began a systemic search through the books, finally stopping at the last one, her finger tapping at a photo. "Here is he. But he's changed since then." She pulled out her phone, taking a photo of the page and sending it on to Frankie. "Frankie needs to know this."

Graeme stood beside her, his finger stopping her from turning the page before he nodded.

"There was always something about him that none of us liked. He wasn't there after that first year. I heard he had been asked to leave." Graeme's eyes raised as he stared across the room, not seeing the photos on the wall that Abe's sister, Rebecca, had placed there. "He was in the church as well. Sue never liked him. Always avoided him if she could."

"That's good to know. I guess the guys will be contacting the college then, won't they?" Kat looked around as the door closed behind her and Frankie stood there, a frown on his face. "Frankie?"

"Darcy?"

She looked up at him, shaking her head. "I'm working on it, Frankie. I'll have your profile soon."

She tapped the yearbook with a slender finger. "He was there, Frankie. All those years ago."

Frankie nodded. "I get that. Graeme, who else have you come up with?"

Graeme stared at him, then almost threw the papers at him. "Here. Dad and I have been working. I'm out of here." They watched, stunned, as Graeme moved quickly past them and was gone. They heard the sound of his truck and just stared at one another.

Graydon shook his head. "You've pushed too far, Frankie. He'll not be back. He'll be out there on his own, looking for her. And I am afraid of what will happen to him if they find him first." Graydon stood, hesitated, and then limped away, his cane tapping in time with his steps.

Chapter 43

Leaning against his truck, his arms extended along the hood, Graeme's eyes moved as he searched the forest on the other side of the lake. She was here, he knew that. She was here somewhere and he planned on finding her, not leaving until he did.

"Where are you, Sue?" His voice was a whisper.

Graeme walked towards the path in front of him, hearing the sounds of the forest coming back to life now that his truck engine was silenced. He studied the path, a frown on his face. Someone had been in and out of here, just recently. He shot a glance behind him and then moved forward.

Coming to a stop, he studied the cabin, not seeing anyone around, but there was a faint trail of smoke, dying away against the afternoon light. Is this where she is, Lord? Is she on her own? Have You protected my lady?

Graeme walked quietly forward, his eyes searching for anyone around him, and not seeing anyone. His hand hesitated as he reached for the door latch before he picked up the stick leaning against the door. He needed something to protect himself, he thought, and this would do just fine.

The door opened silently and he waited, not hearing anything. He searched the main room of the cabin, seeing signs men had been there and were likely to return. His head turning, he walked towards the doors across from him, his hand out as he touched the key in one.

Turning the key, he waited before turning the knob and shoving the door open. Graeme's eyes searched the room, falling to the form on the bed. His stick dropped as he rushed across the room, his hand reaching for Sue. He looked around and then gathered her up in his arms, walking from the room, stopping to close the door and lock it once more.

The cabin door swung closed behind him as he left, his eyes first on Sue and then on the area around him. Sue was gently placed on the front seat of his truck, seatbelt in place, as Graeme stood, a hand resting on her cheek before he was around the truck, behind the wheel, and the truck in motion. He drove away as carefully as he could but as quickly as possible. He didn't see the vehicle stop at the path or the three men that exited, one of them Lewis Blackmore.

Lewis Blackmore was ecstatic. He had Sue back in his clutches once more and this time, she would not escape. He had the paperwork in hand and a bribed justice of the peace with him, ready to marry Lewis to Sue.

He stood, anger growing within him, in the empty bedroom that he had unlocked. He had been assured she was drugged and would not be able to get away from him once more. Spinning, he charged from the room, curses and threats raining down on the man with him. The justice of the peace looked at him and then down at the paperwork, deciding that it wasn't worth it, and walked away.

———

Graeme hesitated once he reached town. He had no idea where to go. He couldn't go to Eddie. He couldn't go to Sue's. And he really didn't want to head back to Abe's. Pulling into a local coffee shop parking lot, he stopped and turned off his truck. Eyes on Sue, Graeme reached for her hand, finding it limp in his grasp.

Drugged, he thought. Sue, what did they do to you? And what were the plans? He searched his memory for what he could do and then pulled away. The church, he thought. Maybe he could get help there. Then he pulled to the side of the road, his phone out, searching for a contact, anyone who could help.

Dave walked towards Graeme as he stood, once more leaning against his truck.

"Graeme? You called? What's up?" Dave saw the hesitation in Graeme and wondered.

"Dave? You're by yourself?"

"That's what you asked for. Now, why?"

"You and your wife, Rylee is it, are good friends of Sue's?"

"We are. Again, why?"

Graeme sighed, knowing he had to speak, but hesitant to. "I found her. She's in my truck. I think she's been drugged. I can't get her to wake up."

Dave peered past him through the open window. "She needs to be at the hospital, Graeme."

"I can't take her there. That's one place they will look for her. I was hoping you could help me, find me some place I can take her to."

Dave paced, and then nodded. "There is. We have a friend from church, John Thompson. He works as an emergency room physician and his wife is a nurse. Let me take you there." He grinned suddenly. "They have helped out my friends on many occasions."

"If it keep her safe, then let's go."

John Thompson stared at the two men standing in his hallway before his eyes dropped to Sue. Mary, his wife, was already heading for the bedroom on the main floor, intent on getting it ready for Sue.

"I won't ask. Follow me." John pointed towards the hallway. "We'll talk later. Graeme, what can you tell me? I know she went missing again."

"She was in a cabin on the other side of the lake from Abe's. Still on his property, I think. I searched, God led me to her, and I found her. I couldn't leave her. Now, I just have to keep her safe."

"You do know you will have to talk to Caleb or Frankie or Eddie, don't you?"

Graeme nodded as he stepped back, his eyes on Sue before they were raised to John, his heart in them for the older man to read.

"I know. Just please? Look her over? I think they drugged her. It just doesn't seem to be a natural sleep."

"I'm sure they did. She wouldn't have stayed this quiet otherwise." John pointed to the door. "Go ahead and help yourself to whatever in the kitchen. Mary had just made fresh coffee and there are muffins and bread out there."

Dave watched Graeme closely, knowing he had just been in hospital himself.

"Graeme? Sit? You need to keep your own strength up."

Graeme sighed as he sat. "Have you talked to anyone? Have you heard anything?"

Dave shook his head, pulling out his phone. "I sent a text message to Caleb, very brief. He'll be by later this morning. He was headed into a meeting he couldn't get out of." He looked up, a smile coming to his face. "Don't worry. Now we have your lady back, we'll keep her safe."

"Can we do just that, Dave? I left Dad and Kat and I think it was Darcy working this morning. Was it only this morning? Anyway, I walked away on them."

Dave laughed. "You wouldn't be the first one to walk away to find your lady. Now, eat."

Chapter 44

His arms crossed, Caleb stood in front of Graeme, a stern look on his face, before his eyes raised to John, who simply shook his head.

"Graeme? Why didn't you call for help to one of us, or at least take her to the hospital?"

"Because I couldn't. Right now, I don't know who to trust. Can you tell me that?" Graeme walked away from Caleb, anger briefly flittering across his face.

"Graeme! Wait. Don't walk away from me. Where exactly did you find her?"

Graeme spun. "In a cabin directly across from Abe's, likely in a direct line from where she was taken. That's how close she was."

Caleb nodded. "We have a team out searching there. But why did you go?"

"Because I felt I had to. God made me go." He spun to stare at John. "You understand, don't you, John?"

"I do, Graeme. Here, sit and talk with Caleb. That's all he's asking of you."

Graeme sat, his eyes on the mug of coffee set in front of him before they raised to Caleb.

"How close are you to finding the men, Caleb?"

"That we are getting closer to." He paused, his eyes down before he looked up. "How close are you to Sue?"

Graeme frowned. "I am not sure what you are asking, Caleb."

Caleb just shook his head. "I am letting you in on something we are investigating. I would say you are invested in Sue, that she is important to you, just by your actions. A patrol office picked up a local justice of the peace out on the highway, He'll lose his license to practice, more than likely. He had been bribed to perform a marriage today. A marriage with Sue as the wife."

Graeme stared at him. "No wonder I felt such a burden to find her. How do we keep her safe?"

Caleb studied him. "I need you to walk through the MacKay house with me or Eddie. There's something there we are missing." He held up his hand. "I know what you and your father were up to. I have been given the list of names. Kat is searching them as is Emma. And yes, Darcy has given me a profile. She has described Lewis Blackmore, but we are sure there is someone else."

"There always is. When did you want me to go through that place?"

"Today. We have a warrant that lets us. John?"

"Sue's still sleeping, Caleb. I have no idea what she was given, but I don't think it will wear off anytime soon. I've sent in bloodwork to try and determine what substance is was. However, it may be just a case of waiting for it to get out of her system.”

“I want this guy, Caleb.” They could see the anger in Graeme and both men prayed for their friends.

An hour later, Graeme stood in the entry of the MacKay house, hesitant to enter, but knowing he had to. Caleb stood on one side, Eddie on the other side of him, watching him closely.

“What exactly are we looking for?” Graeme wasn’t sure what they wanted from him.

“That we’re not sure of. We need you to go through, tell me if something is off, you notice anything different.” Caleb and Eddie exchanged glances. Neither of them were sure what they were looking for.

Graeme wandered the house, his steps sounding loud on the hardwood, softer on the rugs and carpets that had been laid. It looks so different, he thought, with the furniture and furnishings in place. He shook his head as he walked up the steps to the second floor, his eyes searching, although he had no idea what he was looking for.

Back on the main floor, he stood, looking around before he headed for the basement. Even then, he wasn’t sure what to look for. Eddie followed him, Caleb having had to head back to the department for a meeting.

“Graeme?”

“I don’t see anything, Eddie. What am I to be looking for anyway?”

Eddie shrugged. "We have no idea." He frowned, walking towards the back wall of the basement. "What's this?"

"What's what?" Graeme stood, his eyes on the dirt floor, seeing the disturbance. "I don't remember that, Eddie. What has been buried there?"

"Up the stairs, Graeme. I have to call it in."

The two men stood and watched from the outside, Frankie having appeared.

"Eddie?"

"There was an area that was disturbed. Graeme says it's new."

The crime scene tech approached Eddie, beckoning him over, showing him something that had him spinning to stare at Graeme before he nodded.

"Eddie?" Graeme's voice was quiet.

"Graeme, we've found what they wanted. A trove of uncut jewels."

"Jewels?" Graeme's face showed his shock. "How long were they there?"

Eddie shrugged. "Not long, I would say, likely placed around the last day or so you were here."

Graeme shrugged. "It's possible. The house was never locked when I was working and if I was on the second floor, I wouldn't have known who was in and out." He paused, frowning, his thoughts muddled. "But that doesn't make sense, thought. That's not what they were asking." He headed back for the house, Frankie reaching to stop him, his hand out too late.

<hr>

The younger man wandered around the main floor, his eyes on a portrait. He turned to find Eddie and Frankie beside him. "That. That portrait. I saw someone who looks like him around here. Who is that?"

"That's MacKay. You saw someone like him?"

"I did, and I didn't get a good feeling from him." Graeme sighed, his eyes closing. "I think I saw him with Whitmore, or at least, I think I did. Are they working together?"

"You're just now telling us this?" Frankie's voice was incredulous as his hand turned Graeme and directed him back out the door.

"I didn't know, Frankie. How was I to?" Graeme felt anger rising in him and turned and walked away, leaving Frankie staring after him and Eddie shaking his head.

"Frankie? We need Graeme to work with us. Walking off like that? He just left himself open to being abducted again." Eddie was in his car, following Graeme, pulling to the side of the road, his window down. "In you get, Graeme."

Graeme stood, staring ahead, trying to control his feelings, praying for protection for Sue and himself, before he slid into the car. "I won't tolerate being blamed for this, Eddie."

"We know you won't. Frankie can be abrupt, but that's who he is."

"I won't talk to him again, Eddie. I just can't."
He turned to stare out the window. "Please, take me
back to where Sue is."

Chapter 45

Rousing finally, Sue looked around, not sure where she was, staring at the nicely decorated room. This is not where I was, she thought. God, did You rescue me again? Thank you, if You did.

She sat up, her head spinning, before she reached for clean clothes and then a shower, feeling refreshed. Turning as she heard a tap at the door, she stared at Mary as she entered.

"Mary?"

"Sue, you're up and dressed. I imagine the shower felt good." Mary stood in front of her for a moment before reaching to hug her. "Come. I have some food if you want. If not, we have your peppermint tea."

"Mary, where am I?"

"At our place, my dear. Your young man went in and found you, bringing you here." An arm around Sue, Mary walked her to the kitchen, making her sit. "What do you feel like eating?"

"Just some toast, if I could." Sue sighed. "What did Graeme do?"

"He searched the cabins on the other side of Abe's lake, finding you and bringing you here." Mary turned, leaning against the cupboard, watching Sue closely. "You were drugged, Sue. John wasn't sure with what but you seem to have it out of your system."

"It had to have been in the water bottle. That's all I touched or drank from." Sue's head went down on her arms. "Isn't this over with yet?"

"They're working on it. Your young man will be back soon, I suspect. He headed out to Abe's to talk with his father."

Sue nodded. "He's not my young man. And I know he'd do that. Have you heard anything?"

"No, we haven't. But then Caleb and his people wouldn't talk to us." Mary watched as the younger woman nodded.

"No, they won't. I need to call one of them. I know who's behind this. It's not Whitmore, although he's a big part of this."

Mary's hand kept her in her chair. "Eat, Sue, and then we'll call Caleb." She turned as she heard the doorbell, heading that way.

Caleb stood in the kitchen doorway, his eyes on Sue, noting that she was not looking up, not even realizing someone else was there.

"Sue?"

Caleb's voice had Sue jumping, her eyes huge as she looked up at him.

"Caleb? When did you get here?"

"Just now." He accepted the mug of tea offered him as he sat across from Sue. "We need to talk, Sue."

"I know we do. But first, will you pray? I need that. I know it's not over and it's just going to get worse. I have a name for you."

———

214

Caleb nodded, his head bowing as he prayed. He wasn't sure what was going on with Sue, not at that point. He was just glad Graeme wasn't there. He knew what Sue would have to say might just set him off on a hunt on his own.

"Okay, Sue? First, how are you feeling?"

"Sleepy. I don't know what it was I was given, but it had to be in the water." She shuddered. "It was Whitmore, wasn't it?"

"It was. One of our patrol officers picked up a justice of the peace. He had been bribed to perform a marriage."

She sighed. "Mine, right? He just doesn't get it." She shifted uncomfortably in her chair. "What does it take to get him to leave me alone?"

Caleb went to speak, then felt his phone vibrating. He excused himself to look at the text message, his eyes raising to Sue, even as his face tightened with stress.

"Sue?" When she looked up at him, he shook his head. "They just found Whitmore. He's dead."

"Dead? How?"

Caleb just shook his head. "That's all part of an investigation now, Sue. You know I can't tell you."

She sighed. "I know you can't. Does this mean it's over?" She was hopeful.

"Not yet. We need to know why he was so fixated on you. And we need to find whoever it is that is after Graeme."

"He's not safe, is he? Look into people in his past. I know Dad and his father connected years ago, but I can't for sure if that's what it's about." She paused, then said a name and relationship to her, her eyes on Caleb as he studied her and then nodded.

"Your Dad mentioned him, but not why."

"He's been in trouble all his life. Dad never let him around me if he could avoid it. I never went to that house, if there was a chance he was there." Her head went down on her folded arms, a huge sigh drawn from her. "Talk to Dad again."

"We will, Sue. But first, your cases you've been working on? What do you need me to bring here for you? I know you want to be working."

"My laptop. There are a pile of six folders. I need those." She looked up. "Somehow, this is connected to those six, but I can't figure out how." She paused, looked at him. "You found something in the house."

Caleb nodded. "We did. Graeme walked back through with us, but there is nothing to show that he is involved in anything other than painting the house as he was contracted to."

Sue nodded. "I didn't think there would be. It comes back to me, doesn't it? And that person!" She shoved back from the table, anger in her movements. "He's taken years away from me when I couldn't go around people. We need to stop him. How?"

"We'll figure it out, Sue, keeping you safe. Your Mom said she had to head back to their home, something about an appointment she has."

"She does. Dad had planned on staying." She looked around, staring out the back door of the house. "I'm afraid, Caleb. I have never felt fear like I do right now."

Chapter 46

Watching Sue closely, Graeme hesitated to approach her, knowing she was deep in one of her cases. He sighed and then turned and walked away. He didn't think she was even aware of where she was at that point. Caleb had warned him, but he hadn't realized just how deep Sue would sink into her work.

John watched him and then approached him, a quiet word spoken. Graeme nodded, turning once more to watch Sue, and then walked away. He stood for a moment by his truck, studying the house, before he drove away, leaving Sue behind.

Sue looked up an hour later, a frown on her face, before rising. She had heard Graeme, she was sure, but he was nowhere to be found. John stood, watching her search before he spoke.

"He's not here, Sue."

She spun, her eyes on John. "He's not? He was, wasn't he?"

"He was, Sue. He waited in that doorway for you to look up. Graeme wouldn't speak, not wanting to disturb you. When you didn't acknowledge him, he walked away."

"He did? Did he say where he was heading?"

John shook his head. "He didn't. He's in love with you, Sue, just won't tell you. He doesn't want you to feel trapped."

She sighed. "I know he is. I don't want him hurt any more than he has been."

"And you don't think he wasn't by you ignoring him? We all know you delve deep into your work, Sue, but you are recovering. And this time, there is someone else involved." John paused, seeing Eddie hesitating in the hallway. "You need to keep that in mind. You may have driven him away for good."

Sue stared at him, shock and then sorrow on her face. "What did I do, John?"

"You let your humanness take over. You need to learn to trust God, Sue. I know you are a believer, even though a young one. You need to learn to let God have control. Can you do that?"

She finally nodded. "I think I can. He'll have to work with me on that one. Where did Graeme go?"

Sue spun as Eddie spoke. "He's left town, Sue. He told me there was nothing here to hold him. I tried to talk him out of it, but it didn't work. I've spoken with his father. Graydon said he'd talk to him." Eddie's voice grew stern. "You need to talk to him. This is where the crisis begins. We have word that someone wants what he has, only he has nothing. The only thing we can think of that someone wants that he would have is you."

"Me?"

"Yes, Sue. You. Do you know why?"

She nodded. "I do. Dad's on his way in. We need to talk to him and then make plans. John?"

"We'll eat first, Sue. I want in on this. You're not strong enough yet." John just shook his head at her protest. "You're not, Sue. You can hardly keep your eyes open right now. Go. Rest for a bit. Once everyone is here, then we'll eat and then we'll make plans." His eyes met Eddie's, who nodded.

Two hours later, Sue looked around the table, her eyes meeting those of the men gathered there. Caleb, Frankie, Eddie, Abe, her father, Graeme's father, and John all sat waiting for her. Emma was beside her, Kat on her other side. She knew Darcy had left paperwork with Emma.

"Where do we start?"

"At the beginning, Sue, and that goes back a long way, doesn't it?" Caleb's voice was compassionate.

"It does, Caleb. Unfortunately, it does. It goes back to my childhood. Dad?" She searched for her father, finding him beside her, Kat moving away so he could.

"I never knew, love. If I had, I would have done something."

"I know, Dad. Who knew Jamie would be like this?" She named a cousin, one she had been afraid of for years. "What did he do?"

"We'll figure it out. First, we need to keep you safe and away from him. Then, we need to find your young man." Graydon spoke, his eyes on Sue. "I haven't heard from him, and that's unusual."

"He's got him, doesn't he?" Sue's voice shook with fear, before she sighed. "I drove him away today, without meaning to. I drove him right into Jamie's hands."

"We don't know that you did, Sue." Frankie spoke up, before he rose, his phone out to take a call.

Eddie watched him closely, seeing when his face tightened into grim lines and his eyes slid closed. Jamie has him, now doesn't he, Lord? How do we do this? How do we get Graeme away from Jamie but keep Sue safe?

Frankie excused himself, almost running from the house, intent on finding the patrol officer who had discovered Graeme's truck near the MacKay house. This is not what we need, Frankie thought. Lord, can we just get this over with?

Frankie walked through the house, not seeing anything that shouldn't be there. Why was Graeme's truck here? He turned to the responding officer.

"What did you find?"

"This." He held up a bag with a phone in it. "The phone is locked, so I'm not sure if it's Graeme's or not."

Frankie nodded. "What else?"

"There's no sign of a struggle, if that's what you're asking. It's hard to tell if anyone other than Graeme was here. There has to have been. His truck was unlocked, as if he had just stepped from it and pulled out his phone to make a call. No evidence of any foul play."

Frankie sighed. "That's what I thought you would say. Keep working it. This has to be a priority.

———

We have just had word in that there is a contract out of him. It's all related to Sue. He's the one that will be used to reach her."

"Sue?"

"Yeah, Sue. She and Graeme seem to be a couple. Whoever is after Sue will use Graeme."

Chapter 47

Graeme stared at the man in front of him, throwing his phone aside, the pistol held on him letting him know he had no choice. He walked towards the other man, feeling himself shoved towards a vehicle. He climbed behind the wheel as directed, waiting to be told what direction he needed to go. Sighing to himself, he wished he had not come to the MacKay house. Certainly, Graeme had not expected to be taken captive again.

The man, around his age, Graeme thought, motioned for him to pull away, telling him where he wanted Graeme to drive to. There were few words spoken. Parking in front of an automobile wrecking yard, he sat, his mind racing, trying to come up with a way out of the predicament he found himself in.

He was ordered from the truck and then to another truck, this one rusted and in shambles. Graeme drove away in this one, not sure how to get away, but knowing at some point he had to. He had to get to Sue, to save her. He heard the mutterings of the man with him, that Sue would pay.

"What did Sue ever do to you?" Graeme's words broke the silence in the cab of the truck.

"None of your affair. You're only being used to get her to come to me."

"She won't, you know. She just won't."

"She will. I've been watching you two. Sue won't let me kill you." The man's laugh was almost a cackle as he shoved Graeme forward. "Into that chair."

Graeme sat harder than he meant to, the force of the jar sending pain through his body, even as his hands were bound to the chair.

"Sue will come." The man's phone was out, a picture taken, and then sent to Sue. "She'll come. No doubt about that."

The man paced away, not seeing the determination of Graeme's face that he would not win, that Graeme would manage to defeat him and keep Sue safe at the same time.

Sue searched for her phone under the paperwork they had spread out on John's dining room table. Mary had just shrugged as Sue apologized.

"Never a problem, Sue. You should know that. I'll just keep the coffee and tea coming, with food thrown in. Peg Brown is heading our way. You all do what you do best, research, and then arrest." Sue had accepted the hug from Mary before she had turned back to work.

Her hands shaking as she found the phone and swiped a finger across it, she drew in a deep breath, finding Eddie beside her.

"A photo, Sue?"

Sue nodded, handing him her phone. "Of Graeme. I don't recognize the number it came from."

Eddie forwarded it to himself and then walked away, having handed Sue back her phone. He searched for Caleb and Frankie, pulling them aside.

"Sue just received a photo of Graeme. I think I know where he is. The building is familiar looking."

Frankie stared at it. "It is, but I can't think of which one at the moment. Can you?"

The three men studied the photo, but none of them could place the building.

"I have people on the streets watching for him." Frankie turned to find Sue, his eyes assessing his fellow officer. "She's not going to be able to do much more today. She's ready to collapse."

"She won't quit, Frankie. Not unless we make her." Caleb sighed, walking across to Sue, Paul and Graydon's eyes on him. "Sue, we need you to step back for a moment and take a break." She shook her head even as his hand stopped her forward motion. "I'm sorry, Sue. I'll have to pull rank on you and remove you, unless you stop and rest."

Sue sighed. "I know I need to, but I feel I am just so close to finding him, to finding that one piece of evidence we need."

"No, you rest, Sue. Take some time away from this and spend it with God. He'll help you get through this." Caleb studied her face, seeing the fatigue and strain in it. "Graeme won't be hurt. He needs him to get to you."

"I know, Caleb. I know. I am praying that we find something before I have to meet with him. And I know that's what he wants. I just don't know why."

Sue headed for the bedroom she had been using, Emma following, shutting the door quietly behind her as Sue sank to the bed.

"Sleep some, Sue. You need it."

Sue nodded. "I know I do. I just hate this, you know."

Emma sat beside her, an arm around her as she prayed before she rose and walked away, leaving Sue to curl up on the bed, pulling a blanket over her, even as her eyes closed and she slept, a dreamless, deep sleep that she needed.

Emma paced the living room, deep in thought, Abe watching her before he approached her.

"Emma?"

"We're missing someone, something. I don't know what though." She spun. "That profile Darcy did. Where is it?" She reached for it, scanning it quickly before she tapped it. "There is someone behind this man. Who?"

Paul stood watching her before he spoke. "The ones named as his parents are his adoptive parents. Here is the name of the biological parents. Are they behind this?"

Caleb froze as Paul spoke. "Where did we note that he was adopted?"

"We didn't, Caleb. I don't think we knew that." Eddie turned to stare at Paul.

Paul shook his head. "I thought Sue had told you that. I'm sorry."

"Not your fault, Paul. We're pulling in so much information that we're losing track of it all." Eddie looked around as Kat spoke. "What was that, Kat?"

"I saw that. I did a search. Here is the information that you need." She reached for the printer and pulled sheets from it. I've found a lot of information we didn't have."

Paul looked over Eddie's shoulder as he skimmed through it. "It looks as if you've gotten just about everything. I know Sue hated being around him. He turned up at her college, at the church she attended every once in a while. I think this is likely why she never trusted God. She thought He should have protected her and felt that He didn't. Now, where does this take you?"

Caleb turned as he heard a sound from Graydon, watching as Graydon was across the room, his arms around his son. He walked that way, motioning Frankie to the side.

"Talk to me, Frankie."

Frankie had disappeared shortly before that, in response to a call. "My people on the streets found him and rescued him. They also detained Jamie until we got there. I've had Graeme assessed at Emergency. He's fine, just shaken. He needs to talk to us before he talks to Sue. Where is she?"

"Sleeping. I made her step back. We'll need her to stay back now." Caleb watched as Graeme searched for Sue, nodding as his father spoke to him. "We have the names of the biological parents. We're searching for them."

"Caleb?" Graeme stood in front of him. "That was Jamie, Sue's cousin. She never liked him. Neither did I, to tell you the truth. What is going on?"

Chapter 48

Her eyes springing open, Sue stared around at the room she was in, her heart racing. She had dreamt about Jamie and how he had hated her. Why that was, she wasn't sure, and didn't know if anyone could ever tell her. She sat up, shoving the blanket away, disoriented for a moment before she was on her feet, heading for the dining room, a low light snapped on beside her as she searched the paperwork, finding the piece of information that she needed. Sue sighed to herself. It had been here all along. If she had known sooner, maybe none of this would have happened to Graeme or herself, but then she acknowledged that God was sovereign. He could have stopped this way back when it first started, but He didn't. God, I don't know why, but You do. Perhaps I would not have met Graeme, had him become such a part of my life. I don't know where he is right now, but I know I love him, in a way I never thought I would ever love anyone.

Sue turned as she heard a slight noise, her hand going to her chest as her heart jumped in fear. This is ridiculous, she thought. I'm a police officer. I'm not supposed to react like this.

Graeme stood for a moment, watching the lady he loved more than his own life, hurting that she was going through what she was. He wanted this over, wanted to explore a relationship with Sue, to see if she felt the same way. All he knew was that the lady who had his heart was hurting and he couldn't make it better.

"Sue?" Graeme kept his voice low as he moved towards her, a cup of her tea extended to her.

"Graeme? When did you get here?"

"Last evening. Mary said you were sleeping when I pulled in. I hear our Dads have headed towards your town, with some of Abe's men."

"They have? Mom went that way for an appointment. Is she in trouble?"

Graeme just wrapped her in his arms, his chin resting on her head, waiting as she hesitated and then wrapped her own arms around him.

"Where do we stand, Sue?"

She shook her head. "I have no idea, to tell you the truth." Her voice was low, not wanting to wake anyone else. "What happened to you?"

"Jamie."

"Jamie? He found you? How did you get away?" She leaned back to look up at him, seeing his heart in his eyes as he watched her, and feeling content to be held.

"I stopped by the MacKay house. I just wanted to sit and think about it. He was there. Made me throw away my phone. It was bizarre how he made me drive away in his truck, ending up at a wrecking yard, and then driving away from there to a building in town. I think it was some of Frankie's people who came in and got me out and then held onto him for the police to arrive. He's in jail right now, Sue, facing charges here but I understand he has murder charges and kidnapping charges elsewhere."

Sue shuddered. "I never felt safe around him. He's not the one in charge, though." She pushed away from him, to reach for the paper she had found. "This is why. It was here along, Gray. We missed it."

"No, we didn't miss it. You weren't ready for it. None of us were. God's timing is perfect."

She studied him, seeing the peace he had. "How do you do that, Graeme? How are you so peaceful?"

He shrugged. "I guess because God has given me that peace."

She nodded. "I'm getting there, I think. But this? Jamie was adopted. I don't know if I ever told you that."

"You did, back when you told me you didn't want him around you."

"I told you that?"

"You did, just after we became friends. I tried my best to keep him away. I could see his character. It didn't show with his parents, but it did with you. Now, why?"

Sue shrugged. "I have no idea, but we need to plan something to bring him out. Caleb won't let me. I've sent him a message, asking for some vacation time starting today. I need it."

"You're not working on this without me. What are you planning?" He drew out a chair and made her

———

sit, taking a chair beside her and reaching for her hands. "What do we do to bring out his parents?"

"That's what I was trying to decide. What are your thoughts?"

They finally reached an agreement as to how they would proceed, knowing that Caleb and her fellow officers wouldn't let her but knowing they had to put themselves out there, to become targets. That was the only way they could do this, they thought. Graeme prayed for them as they made their decision, asking for safety and protection, and that it would soon be over for Sue.

Chapter 49

Eddie stared at Caleb the next morning, not quite sure he had heard him right. He looked down the hallway behind him, seeing Sue's door still shut.

"She did what?"

"She asked for some vacation time. Frankly, she needs it. But I just know they're working on this." Caleb was frustrated.

"I know they are. They likely have a plan." He turned as Frankie walked towards them, shaking his head.

"Did you know that Sue and Graeme are out and about?" Frankie was just a little angry at Sue.

"I know they are, Frankie. Sue asked for some vacation time. I let her have it. She's burning out right now, going through what she is, and with the workload she has. She'll be back in a week." Caleb turned and walked away, his thoughts muddled for once. He wasn't sure Sue was making a good decision, though.

Frankie turned to Eddie, finding the older detective lost in thought. "Eddie?"

"Frankie, I think I know how we can work this. Sue and Graeme are going to put themselves out there, as a couple, I suspect. Let's you and I find them and see what their plans are."

———

"I wish I could, Eddie, but I have court this morning. You can talk some sense into them."

Eddie watched Sue and Graeme as they headed for Mac's, a local diner, before he followed them, watching the man who had been intent on their progress along the street. He searched his memory and nodded. It was Whitmore's biological father. He pulled out his phone, asking for assistance, knowing that it had just became more dangerous for his two friends.

Although he was just behind them, when Eddie reached the diner, he couldn't see them. He paused, a puzzled look on his face. Mac approached him, his head tilted to study his friend.

"Eddie?"

"Mac. Sue and Graeme? Did they come in?"

Mac turned to study the diners. "No, I don't think they did. If they did, they left right away."

Eddie groaned. "Then, he's got them. Where would he take them?"

"What are you talking about, Eddie?" Mac paled at Eddie's words.

"Jamieson. He's got them. Now to find them. Mac, if you see him or them, call the station. It's a matter of life and death for them." Eddie left on the run, heading for Caleb, and then his car, intending on searching the area.

Caleb watched closely as Doug and his ETF team approached a building.

———

"How sure are we, Eddie?"

Eddie shrugged. "I'm not that sure. We have a lot of buildings to search." He squinted at the sun. "It's been four hours since I saw them. They could be dead, or taken out of town."

Doug walked towards them, shaking his head. "Not here, Eddie. Where now?"

Eddie sighed. "I was hoping they would be. That's what my sources said." His voice died away as his gaze shifted. "Doug. That building behind. It's on the same property, isn't it?"

Doug spun. "It is. Let me take me team in."

Doug's team spread out, finding entrances to the building and moving forward on silent feet, hearing voices in front of them. Tom, the second in command, watched Doug closely, seeing as he paused and then moved forward once more.

They waited and then moved in, hearing a sharp cry from Sue, a call from Graeme and then silence. Tom had the man down, even as Doug's feet carried him forward, reaching for Graeme and then moving him with help to reach for Sue.

"Caleb?" Tom ran for the chief. "We have them. They're hurt, but we have the man as well."

Caleb ran that way, Eddie and Frankie with him, even as he saw Dave and his partner and another team of paramedics heading towards the building.

"Is the man alive?"

"Yes. Now maybe we can get answers for Sue."

———

Chapter 50

That morning, Sue had walked away from John's home, her hand tight in Graeme's. He tucked her into her car, walking around to slide behind the wheel, a prayer rising. This would be the day, he thought, the day it ends. Lord, protect my lady. Don't let anything happen to her.

They had agreed to a plan, not letting anyone else know. John had shaken his head at them, telling them they needed a backup, someone to watch out for them. They had exchanged a glance and then shaken their heads at him, telling him they wouldn't put anyone at risk.

Graeme's steps had slowed as he felt Sue tugging on his hand during their walk towards Mac's, a question on his face as he looked down at her before he looked up. He didn't know the man in front of them, but Sue seemed to.

"Sue?"

"Graeme, meet Rick Jamieson. Jamie's natural father." Sue's steps had stopped as she watched the man in front of her, seeing what Jamie would have looked like in a few years.

"Move, you two. Around the diner. You're not stopping in there today." Jamieson had a weapon pointed at Sue.

Graeme's hand had tightened on Sue's as they walked away from the diner, his eyes in constant motion to try and find a way to escape. He had sensed Sue go into her work mode, and wondered at that. They were finally shoved into a building, one he had seen before and wondered how he knew it. Then, he remembered. It had been a picture in the MacKay house, just a small painting that he had glanced at and then moved away from.

"All right, Jamieson. Now that you have our attention, what do you want?" Sue's voice was stern.

"What do I want? Nothing, lady. Absolutely nothing. I was asked to find you and I have. The one who wants you will be here soon."

Sue shook her head. "Not buying that, Jamieson. I saw your record. You work alone."

"Not this time. There really is someone else out there." He paced, his weapon wavering from them and then back.

He's dangerous, Sue thought. She studied him, trying to find a way to take him down and not seeing one. She moved slightly, away from Graeme, seeing his frown, and then she pointed between the two of them. Seeing his acknowledge by the slight nod, she turned her attention back to Jamieson, watching him closely.

He's a loose cannon, Sue thought. One wrong move and we'll be dead. Lord, if that happens, let it be me that goes. Keep Graeme safe.

———

Jamieson didn't speak, growing more agitated over the hours he waited, pacing towards the door and then back, his eyes first on Sue and then Graeme. Sue was growing tired of this. She wanted it over. A small step on her part took her towards the door and towards the man. Taking him down would be difficult but she had to do something.

A sound at the entrance had Jamieson turning that way and Sue lunged towards him, her hands on his wrist, fighting him for the weapon. Graeme stood for a second and then threw himself into the melee. Jamieson went down under their onslaught, Sue's grin on his wrist finally shaking the weapon loose. She kicked at it, her grasp on his wrist momentarily weakened. He took advantage of that, sending her flying, to lay still before he turned to Graeme, a blow to his jaw sending him backwards before Jamieson reached for a pipe, the pipe landing heavily on Graeme's shoulder, sending him to the floor and into darkness.

Jamieson rose, breathing heavily, his hand holding the pipe, ready to strike again. He shook his head. This wasn't supposed to happen. They were to play nice, he thought, and wait respectfully. He just should have known that woman wouldn't do that.

He spun as he heard footsteps, facing the ETF officers as they entered, the pipe dropping from his hand with a dull clang before he was on the floor and his hands cuffed behind him.

Doug stared at him before his attention went to Sue and he was on his knees beside her, his head dropping in thankfulness as he found her alive before he looked at Tom, who nodded. Both were alive but hurt.

Caleb paced the waiting room at the hospital, his thoughts on his friends, his prayers raising. He knew his wife, Hannah, was around, likely in the chapel, he thought. Eddie paced beside him.

"Caleb? What do we know about this man?"

Caleb shrugged. "Nothing good, I suspect. He's been in town here for years, in the construction business. Grace is looking into him but her preliminary report states that he's been suspected of shoddy work. No one has come forward to accuse him. I think we'll find he's been involved in a lot more than that."

"And you would be right." Frankie stood in their way, stopping their progress. "People are starting to come forward. Emma's working her magic as is Jace. They need to stop throwing information at us."

Caleb grinned as did Eddie. "She won't, you know. Not when it's friends." He turned as he heard his name called.

"Caleb? Any word?" Graydon and Eliza stood beside him, Paul and Eunice behind them.

"Not yet. John's working today. He said he'd be out shortly."

The two couples nodded, turning to find a seat, before Paul and Graydon once more approached them.

"Caleb, what can you tell us?" Graydon was worried, more worried than he had been.

———

"It was Jamie's natural father, Rick Jamieson. He said he was holding them for someone else. At least, that's what Sue was able to say. She was awake for a bit, but I'm not sure if she still is."

"Jamieson? He tried to take over my company years ago. I finally had to get an order against him." Paul turned at a sound from Graydon.

"He did the same to me. I wish I could have stopped him."

"No one could. He had it too well hidden." Eddie looked past them. "There's John, Graydon. I'm not sure which one of you couples that he's looking for."

Chapter 51

Three weeks later, Graeme stood, his eyes on Sue as she wandered her backyard. She had not had any physical injuries but he knew she was struggling mentally and emotionally from what they had gone through. He adjusted the sling he was wearing, a broken collar bone his only physical injury. He hurt for his lady.

Walking down the back steps and then towards Sue, he squinted at the sky. It was coming up to twilight, a time of day he loved, ready to set aside his chores and relax. He could heard the night birds getting set to bring out their chorus even as the chirping and singing of the day birds quietened. He could heard the frogs from a nearby pond and felt content at Sue's.

Sue watched him approaching her, her thoughts muddled. She had talked to Caleb. She wasn't sure if she wanted to continue as a detective. This had taken a lot from her, she thought, that and the shooting where she almost lost her life.

Graeme stood for a moment before he reached to draw her to him, cradling her close to him, feeling her arms hugging him back. They stood before he turned them towards the back of the yard, when Sue had set up a swing. Graeme set it into motion once they were seated.

"Did you talk to Caleb?"

"I did. He said he'd have a conversation with us later, but they have everyone. There was no one else other than Jamieson." She sighed, her head going down on his shoulder. "It goes back to Mom, did you know? He was fascinated with her, wanted to date her. She refused and walked away. He didn't like that and planned revenge."

"Was he the one behind Blackmore?"

"No, that monster came up with that idea on his own. I never liked him. Now I know why."

"Jamieson has a lot to answer for, doesn't he?"

"He does. Eddie talked to me earlier today, as well. He's going back through Jamieson's work here in town. There have been a lot of corners cut, shoddy work. It's a nightmare." Her head twisted on his shoulder as she looked up at him. "Graeme, how does he connect with your people?"

"I talked to Dad. He wanted to take over Dad's company and good name a few years ago. Dad thinks now it was to cover what he was up to. I'm not sure we'll ever know what all he was involved with. Frankie said he's the one who had Peter killed."

"That's so sad. Such depravity. But that's what sin does, doesn't it?"

Graeme nodded before his chin rested on her hair. "It does. God has been good to us, my love. And that's what you are. My love."

Sue stilled her motions. She had been rubbing a hand along her jeans, not sure what to say next.

"I am?"

Graeme searched her face. "You have been since college. I missed you when you went away. I didn't know where you were. I was so afraid I'd meet you one day and you would have found a love and been married."

Sue stared at him before her face softened. "That wouldn't have happened, Graeme."

He stared down at her, seeing her answer in her face. "It wouldn't have?"

"No, it wouldn't have. I tried to get away from you, from your God. He wouldn't let me. I felt like He just held out His hand one day and I took hold of it. When I was shot and almost died, I saw Him. He was in my hospital room, the whole time I was there. One of His angels stood at the head of my bed."

Graeme's arms tightened on her. "He will do that." He paused, lost in thought. "Sue, will you be mine? Be the part of my heart I have been missing?"

She looked up at him. "I will." She groaned.

"Now what?"

"You know, when we tell anyone, they'll say they knew it."

Graeme laughed. "Let them. We are a team, my love, a team that will go forward in God's strength." He was silent for a moment. "Dad wants to change the company to a consulting company. I like that idea."

"So do I. Would you work from here?"

He nodded. "We will. Dad and Mom have found a house they are purchasing. Mom said she knew I would never return to my home town." His eyes searched her face. "But what about you?"

"Me?"

"Yes, you. Will you still be a detective?"

She shrugged. "I am not sure, Gray. I think not. This has taken too much from me. When I spoke with Caleb this afternoon, he asked me the same thing, then told me to take some time and decide what I wanted to do. He was fine with it if I decided I didn't want to."

Graeme's arms tightened on her. "Then, that's what you do." He bent, his lips meeting hers in a kiss. "We'll work through this together."

Sue was on a search. She couldn't find her husband of three weeks, even though she had heard his voice raised in song earlier. Now, where is he, she wondered? She jumped as she felt arms come around her.

"Looking for something, sweetheart?" Graeme's voice was low in her ear.

"I was. Your parents want us to come for dinner tonight. I know it's short notice and all." She turned in his arms, her eyes on him.

He shrugged. "We can, if that's what you want to do."

"I do. Your parents are just too funny at times. I love being around them."

An hour later, Sue and Graeme stood inside the door at his parents, staring at them and then Sue's parents, their gaze moving towards their friends.

"Mom?" Graeme's voice held a question.

"We wanted to do this, as a thank you to your friends, and Sue's fellow detectives. Sue, your parents did as well. Do you mind?"

Sue shard a look with Graeme and then with her parents. "Not at all. We had talked about doing something like this, but hadn't finalized anything."

"Oh, dear, we've stepped on your toes." Eliza's face held a look of distress.

"Not at all, Mom. Not at all. We appreciate your doing this. We'll do something later. Right now, let's mingle and then eat."

Caleb stood watching his friends before he approached Graeme. "Graeme, how are you really doing?"

"We're getting there, Caleb. We're getting there. It will take time, but we'll get through this." He grinned. "A question for you? How are you going to manage without Sue in the office?"

Caleb shook his head, even as he grinned. "We're not really losing her, you know. She'll be working with both Emma and Kat. I just know she'll make a lot of work for us."

"That she will." Graeme reached to hug his wife to him, watching at Hannah approached Caleb. "Thank you for all you did. I know it was difficult, being one of your officers. Has everything been sorted out?"

"It has, finally. It was what we thought. Revenge on your parents, Sue. Trying to keep his deeds undercover here. He's the one who had the jewels buried at the MacKay house. He was trying to frame you."

"That's about what I figured." Graeme's voice died away, his eyes not seeing the crowd of friends in front of him. "God has been so good, Caleb. He

---

protected us. Protected Sue all these years. Brought her to Himself. What more could we ask for?"

"That He has, my friend. Listen, we need to run, but you'll be around for dinner one day next week?"

"That we will." Graeme studied Sue, watching her closely, seeing the relaxation on her face that hadn't been there. "Doing okay, sweetheart?"

"I am, my love. I didn't think I would marry, but God had plans for us, plans He hadn't shared."

"That's what Murphy always says, that God has plans and purposes we don't know about. I'm glad you're retiring from the force. You'll miss it but you'll find your niche."

"God does that, doesn't he?"

"Does what?"

"Moves us on to where and what He wants us to be."

Graeme agreed silently, knowing how far Sue had come in her walk with God. He held the love of his life in his arms, content to let her walk forward with God, even if she did that on her own. That's how God works, he thought, a praise raising from his heart.

Dear Readers

Thank you for choosing Sue and Graeme's story. I had no intention of writing Sue's story. She was a secondary character in the Riverville books, but she was demanding, telling me I had to write her story.

Going through their adventure, Sue learned she needed to depend on God. That He was the one who was there. Graeme had to relearn this as well.

God is there for us, whether we know it or not. He is present with us every day, every moment. His hand leads us forward in our walk with Him.

During the writing of this for Camp Nanowrimo in April, 2020, we are in the midst of the COVID-19 pandemic. God is still in control, even though it seems He's not. Put your hand in His and walk with Him.

God bless.

Ronna

www.ingramcontent.com/pod-product-compliance
Lightning Source LLC
Chambersburg PA
CBHW061237210726
48293CB00003B/799